# FAE'S DREAM
## FATED MATES OF THE FAE ROYALS, SUMMER COURT BOOK 6
## HELEN WALTON

Walton House Publishing

# CONTENTS


Foreword                                          1

Epigraph                                          3

1.  Aislinn                                        4

2.  Fallon                                        13

3.  Aislinn                                       23

4.  Fallon                                        32

5.  Aislinn                                       41

6.  Fallon                                        47

7.  Aislinn                                       56

8.  Fallon                                        62

9.  Aislinn                                       68

10.  Fallon                                       77

11.  Aislinn                                      89

12.  Aislinn                                      99

13.  Fallon                                      106

14.  Aislinn                                      112

15. Fallon     120

16. Aislinn     130

17. Fallon     141

18. Aislinn     147

19. Fallon     155

20. Aislinn     162

21. Fallon     171

22. Aislinn     183

23. Aislinn     192

24. Fallon     200

25. Aislinn     207

26. Aislinn     215

27. Fallon     222

28. Aislinn     231

29. Fallon     241

30. Aislinn     250

31. Aislinn     258

32. Fallon     264

Acknowledgments     267

Also By     268

About Author     270

# FOREWORD

AUTHOR NOTE

Choosing character names is not always easy, and there are times you pick them to mean something for the character and the story. I've included the pronunciation and meaning of the names, and if you're like me, and like to know and still pronounce the names the way you read them, then welcome to my club.

Niamh pronounced neeve meaning radiance.

Fintan pronounced fin-tan meaning white fire.

Eamon pronounced aim-on meaning keeper of riches.

Maeve pronounced may-veh meaning intoxicating.

Diarmuid pronounced deer-mid meaning without enemy.

Orlaith pronounced or-lah meaning golden princess.

Rian pronounced ree-an means little king.

Briana pronounced bree-a-nah meaning noble.

Aislinn pronounced ash-lin meaning a vision or dream.

Saoirse pronounced seer-sha meaning freedom.

Lorcan pronounced lor-can meaning silent or fierce.

Ciara pronounced kee-ra meaning dark.

Roisin pronounced row-sheen meaning little rose.

Donagh pronounced done-acka meaning brown-haired warrior.

Deirdre pronounced deer-dree meaning broken-hearted.

Malachi pronounced mal-lah-key means messenger of God.

Fallon pronounced fa-len meaning descended from a ruler.

Ailbhe pronounced all-bay meaning white.

Tadhg pronounced tie-guh meaning poet or philosopher.

Eabha pronounced ey-ya meaning life.

For the truth of love lies in the dreams of passion.

# CHAPTER ONE
# AISLINN

ALL THE HAPPY LOVE going around my family lately was torture. I didn't begrudge my brothers and sisters finding their fated mates. Or perhaps I did.

My finger rubbed the edge of the blade strapped to my thigh. I let the feeling I could defend myself against anything soothe me. Over and over, my finger stroked the dagger until I was confident I could at least pretend to be happy for them all. I stood before the sentiment gave way to the churning emotions that never seemed to leave me. Everyone's eyes landed on me, and the polite conversation halted. My brother, Lorcan, tensed, his muscles bunching beneath his clothes, as he inched closer to his newly found fated mate, Pepper. A witch, no less. I'd never harm her, even if her species had played a hand in the deaths of my grandparents.

"I need to pack and prepare to leave the Summer Court," I said.

"There is no hurry," Father said, running an observant gaze over my twitching fingers.

"Our lives depend on us curing the spring." My fingers tightened on the hilt as if I'd kill whatever was ailing our Spring of Life with the tiny blade. If only it were that easy.

"Aye." Father nodded, sending his crown of thorns into writhing agitation around his head. "It troubles me more than you all seem to think."

He shifted as though ready to stand, but Mother placed a calming hand on his arm. The look my parents shared was one of pure, unadulterated love and understanding. We'd all grown up with that type of love as an example for hundreds of years. We all aspired to find that type of love, too. And now my two brothers and two of my sisters had found their mates. Fated mates, no less. The one meant for us and us alone.

"Aislinn," Mother said, standing too. "I'll accompany you to your room. With luck, Briana will return with her mate, and you can meet him before you go on your journey."

That was another thing bothering me. I believed I was close to my siblings, yet Briana and Lorcan had kept the fact they'd found their fated mates a secret from me. I didn't care that they weren't supposed to be on Earth.

They should have told me, but I supposed I kept my secret too. They all wondered why I was angry all the time.

If only they understood the reason.

If they comprehended I'd lost what they now had, they'd pity me. Better to have their confusion about my attitude than to have them act like I was breakable. I wasn't. The torture I'd experienced at the hands of the Trappers hadn't broken me. I'd never break.

I tossed back my head, flinging the thick braid of hair over my shoulder. Mother slid her arm through mine. The contact jolted me out of my whirling thoughts. We walked through the outside doorway and inside the palace, leaving my father and siblings on the terrace in the late afternoon sunshine streaming from the cloudless blue sky. The sunbeams followed us as we made our way inside the doors, warming our backs. As our footfalls sounded on the floor, drawing us deeper into the depths of the palace, we passed servants scurrying through the halls. Probably preparing for a feast or one of my parents' favored balls. Dia, I hoped they weren't about to throw another ball. There'd been so many of late after an absence of the parties for many years.

Mother's fingers rubbed relaxing strokes along my arm, but she said nothing to me, just kept her calming presence at my side. We stopped outside the solid timber of my bedroom door. I waited for Mother to let go, but she stood patiently as though she expected me to invite her in.

Sighing, I opened the door, and we walked into my bedroom. The covers on my bed were a knotted mess, as they were every day. I didn't see the point in making the bed when I'd toss and turn all night anyway the next night. Sunlight streamed through the window across the timber floor in golden beams that made the room welcoming. The woven rug of deep purples shining under the sun's beams was my favorite place to contemplate my life. The wrong choices I'd made. If I laid there now, would Mother sing one of her songs? Would she use the unusual power in her voice to soothe me?

If only I was a young child again, without the knowledge I held in my many centuries of living, then a simple song would cure all my ailments, including my broken heart.

Mother slid her arm from mine and settled on the edge of my bed, made from the twisted branches of a golden tree. It produced memories of Mother brushing my long hair as a child and then braiding it into intricate knots on top of my head. I'd always run through the forest or the crops as a child and had leaves and twigs stuck in my tresses. She'd called me her wild girl. I'd preferred nature to the ballroom. Still did.

I opened my armoire and stared at the contents. I had no clue what to pack for a visit to Earth. Like my eldest siblings, I'd sometimes escaped through the locked Veil to Earth without Father's knowledge, but they had been fleeting visits. Nothing that required luggage.

"Aislinn, talk to me."

I turned from the sight of the many plain dresses. My requirements for the seamstresses. No fancy frills or embroidered fabrics. No pretty flowers or gold stitching. But they must all have carefully concealed slits where I could access my daggers with ease. And the dresses needed to hide the fact I had daggers strapped to my body in various places.

"What would you like me to say?"

"What is on your mind?"

"An awful lot."

"Now is your chance to air your thoughts." She waved her hand delicately around the room. "'Tis you and I here, no one else."

I hauled in a deep breath. "How can you all accept the witch so easily?"

"We do so because Lorcan is our son, and fate sent him a witch as a fated mate. Who are we to disagree with fate?"

"That's the other thing." I paced across the room. "How did she survive his mating mark?"

Mother frowned. "It is a good question, and one we don't know the answer to, but your brother wouldn't transport anyone into the Summer Court that he didn't trust. You are aware of what he and your father did to ensure our safety."

"Aye." I paused at the window and gazed across the rose garden outside.

Long ago, after humans had attacked us and burned us alive, Father and Lorcan had destroyed them. Then Father had sealed the Fae inside the Summer Court.

Now we were dealing with those repercussions of staying locked away. Our Spring of Life was languishing, our birthrate too, and finding a fated mate was nigh on impossible. Now that my brothers and sisters had found their fated mates on Earth, Father had created a doorway for the Fae to travel safely with the added protection of guards as escorts to Earth.

"Out of everyone, don't you think Lorcan would make certain a witch was trustworthy?"

"Can we ever trust witches? They sell their potions and spells to the highest bidder."

"Their ways are not for us to question." Mother clasped her hands in her lap. "You realize every supernatural creature has its own ways."

"She's not supernatural, though."

"Well, she must be to survive a Fae mating mark."

Mother pursed her lips. The only sign she was getting annoyed with me. No matter what I threw at my mother, she was always the calm voice in the storm of my emotions.

"Now, what else is bothering you?"

I unsheathed one of my daggers and tossed it at the target hanging on my wall. Everyone else hung my youngest sister Roisin's paintings in their bedrooms. Not me. I'd adorned my walls with targets. Throwing knives was the only thing that calmed me.

"Better?" Mother raised an eyebrow.

"No." I huffed.

Everything was bothering me. The fact Lorcan had returned with a witch as his fated mate was the least disturbing. The mystical messages from Saltine were even more worrisome. What did the witch seer know that we didn't? Could she see our demise to the exact day? Is that what she meant by me finding my fate? And by saying it was almost time for Mother? For Mother to do what exactly was a question I kept pondering.

"What did Saltine mean when she said it's almost time?"

Mother's face flickered with a range of emotions before she smoothed it into a mask of perfect calm. "I canna say."

"Does Father know?"

Her face paled. "No."

"You're scared," I noted.

Mother peered at her clasped hands in her lap. "I'm concerned, aye. Decisions aren't easy to live with. Do we ever know if we made the right choice at the time? We'd never see how things would work out if we'd made a different choice, but Saltine has the gift of sight, so she must see."

"You believe in our old witch seer?"

"Aye. She helped us in the past."

I crossed my arms over my chest. "Why wouldn't she have warned us about the Trappers, then?"

"I canna answer that. Only she can." She lifted her gaze. "But I have to believe my parents died by the Trappers' hands because if they hadn't, something worse would have happened."

"What could be worse?"

"If I'd lost my children," Mother whispered.

Our gazes met and held. Her eyes glistened with unshed tears. I rolled my head to the side. I had so much anger, yet Mother, who should have rage, only had acceptance this was her fate.

"Please be careful on Earth. Your brother and sisters have mentioned it's not the same place we used to frequent."

"No, it's not." I strode back to the armoire and yanked a handful of dresses from the inside. Did it even matter what I wore?

"So, you all were sneaking behind our backs?" Mother's voice firmed, as though she was about to reprimand me.

"Except for Ciara and Roisin. They've never stepped foot on Earth. We understood what we were doing, Mother, and we were careful. We had to search for a cure for the spring's problems."

"Aye, your father can't go on much longer as he has."

I paused in the process of emptying my armoire to glance over my shoulder at her choice of words. "What do you mean?"

She cleared her throat. "I'll see if Briana has returned," she said, standing. "I'm intrigued to see who her fated mate is."

My hand fiddled with a dress in the armoire. "I can't image what he's like. Briana was so in love with her chosen mate that I never considered she'd recover from losing him or her daughter."

"She lived through my worst nightmare. I'm proud of her. I would not have survived such a loss."

"You would have, Mother. You're strong."

She stepped closer and cupped my cheek. "You're strong too. Too strong sometimes. You need to let the ones who love you help you sometimes. That's the way love works."

Love for my family, I understood. Love for my fated mate, I didn't understand. He'd never given me the chance to understand him. It was too late for me to love my fated mate. He was gone forever. I'd had my chance at love and lost it.

I gulped back the building emotion in my throat. "Could you send someone up with a travel case?"

Mother nodded and left the room. Alone, I replayed our conversation in my head so I wouldn't focus on what I'd lost. Many things didn't add up. I'd get to the bottom of them even if I had to threaten everyone with my daggers.

# CHAPTER TWO
# FALLON

Sᴡᴇᴀᴛ ᴀɴᴅ ʙʟᴏᴏᴅ ᴅʀɪᴘᴘᴇᴅ from my face. My sister Erin shook her head while handing me a towel. I wiped my face, closing my eyes for a moment behind the sanctuary of the fabric. Each punch had been brutal, but I'd won in the end.

"It was a close match," Rory said.

"Yes, you're getting slow as the years go by," Erin piped in with her pipsqueak voice.

Even though she was hundreds of years old, she was still my little sister.

As I lowered the towel, I raised an eyebrow. "Are you calling me old?"

"No." Erin's lips twitched as she smothered a giggle before she slammed a hand over her mouth.

Rory smiled at Erin, all doe-eyed and in love. It made me sick. Not because she was my sister, but because of love itself.

I tossed the towel in the basket, noting the red smear across the white fabric. It'd been a while since an opponent had almost bested me. I was the best bare-knuckle fighter in the underground belly of London. Unfortunately, that meant we'd almost worn out our welcome in England. If I became too well-known, then it would make it harder to disappear, even if we lived a long drive from the bustling city on the outskirts of the Linton countryside village.

Hamish, my right-hand man and friend for many years, burst through the changing room door, took one look at my battered face, and shook his head.

"It's time we moved on," he said.

I'd known it was coming. We'd been in the area for over ten years. It would be hard to explain how none of us aged. If we stayed any longer, we'd risk humans and other supernatural creatures questioning what we were. We couldn't risk being discovered. Plus, we were all eager to return to our homeland. Not only to Ireland but also our hometown and the one place we all sensed peace. There was a garden and fountain at the edge of the village that always eased my powers. I longed to return to the place to feel that calmness once again.

"Soon," I agreed.

Logically, I understood it was time, but there was this intuition in my chest that I was supposed to be here. In this place. At this moment in time. For a reason. One I couldn't fathom. The bruises and cuts would heal too fast for me to pretend to be human. I'd have to stay hidden for the time it would take a human to heal before I could show my face in the local village or the fight club again. Everything was getting too risky.

Not to mention the fact Erin was smitten with Rory.

And Rory was human.

He wasn't a Fae.

No matter how much she liked the young man, it didn't matter for she'd outlive him, and how would she explain that to Rory? As I resisted the urge to rub my forehead, I stood and shrugged on a jacket, then tugged on gray tracksuit pants. A far cry from the clothes we used to wear, but that was so long ago.

We'd been stuck on Earth for a lot longer than we'd imagined.

The Fae King's relentless protection of our homeland had left us stranded. Alone, without the help of our leader. My fingers curled into tight fists. I'd love the chance to punch him in the face for forsaking us. For leaving us. And me with no way to get to my fated mate.

For she was a Fae Princess. A beautiful woman with silvery blonde hair. A flower crown adorning the silky strands. The night I'd found her burned and in pain, she'd been beautiful even then. I'd heard of the beauty of the Fae royals, but I'd never met one, not until her. Until she was in my arms, clinging to me as though I was already the greatest love of her life. And I'd ruined it by running after my sister. I'd left my fated mate in the safe hands of her brother, his crown of thorns swirling with agitation as he'd stormed through the area searching for his sister. While I understood his anxiety, I had to find mine. Family mattered, but if I'd known I'd lose centuries with my fated mate, I would have done things differently that night.

The agony of the knowledge of the past seared through my heart every single heartbeat of every day and made the fury inside me build to the point I either had to release it through physical violence or my powers would surge.

I couldn't explain the way I controlled electricity to people if they saw me use my powers. Nor the surge of sparkling Fae power in my hands. I probably had enough electricity to power the entire planet, so I needed to keep that a secret. Otherwise, I'd end up in a laboratory somewhere. I'd heard rumors of that happening to other creatures. Although humans called them aliens, I suspected they were, in fact, supernatural creatures. Even though we'd kept ourselves hidden amongst the humans, it was easy enough to hear the rumors of what people didn't believe existed anymore. Rumors of werewolves and vampires ran rampant, also witches. Everything that existed had a story to it in the human world. Humans believed the stories were pretend.

Erin's bottom lip wobbled as she ducked her head and turned her shoulder to us so we wouldn't see the tears building in her eyes. She grasped how it had to be. I didn't understand how she always let herself get attached to people when she realized we'd have to move on in the end.

"Rory, thanks for coming." I held out my hand.

Rory shook my hand. His grip was firm and a tad sweaty, or perhaps that was my sweat greasing our palms. What I wouldn't give for the refreshing dip in the lake back at our camp.

I swung my arm over Erin's shoulders. She ducked out of my hold and wrinkled her nose.

"Gross."

"I'll rub my sweaty armpit in your face."

Erin rushed to the door and almost ran outside into the blowing gale. Her hair caught in the gust and whipped around her head, making me think about the only time I'd seen my fated mate. A breeze of her own making had swirled around us as though she couldn't control her powers upon our meeting.

Mine had rushed to the forefront, ready to place a mating mark on her chest, but the timing had been horrendous. Neither of us could have afforded to be unconscious in the Quiet while our enemies were burning us alive. Still... the biggest regret of my life. If I'd marked her, would we have lived? At least if I'd marked her, I could track her. As it was, I wasn't sure if she'd survived that night. All I could do was dream she was alive and living locked away in the Summer Court. That was the one notion that kept me going all these lonesome years.

Erin left Rory staring after her longingly. Hamish and I exited the underground boxing ring. We might not be back after tonight, and that weird sensation in my chest tightened. Erin glared at us as she stood beside the sedan. A car that blended in with every other car on the road. Everything we did, we tried to blend into the background as much as possible. We didn't want to draw attention to ourselves. It was why we'd become Travelers at the time they locked us from the Summer Court. Back in those days, their way of living let them hide in the countryside and we needed that anonymity. Now, though, it was less heard of, but we enjoyed the nomadic lifestyle, the way we were left alone by humans who didn't understand the joy of living the way we did.

Hamish clicked the button on the remote control for the car. The orange lights flashed as the car unlocked, and Erin yanked the door open, disappearing into the dimly lit space of the interior.

"I don't understand her."

Hamish grunted. He had a sister himself, so I would have considered he'd be more helpful, but he climbed into the driver's seat, leaving me alone in the cold, dark night. I was always alone. Or that's how it felt.

My sore fingers ached as I opened the car door. The cracks on my split knuckles reopened and oozed fresh droplets of blood. I slid onto the soft leather seats. The car might be nicer than others, but just because we'd been stranded and hiding our supernatural abilities, it didn't mean we hadn't amassed the money and means to live comfortably over the centuries.

Even my bones were weary. Tiredness down to my core filled me. I slid the belt into place, noting the way the skin was knitting itself back together already with my accelerated healing. The car rolled forward through the parking lot. I rested my forehead on the window. Maybe my fated mate was out there. Maybe she wasn't.

I'd never give up the dream that one day I'd find her again.

As the car hit the streets, derelict buildings whizzed by the window as Hamish sped the car through the worst part of town. The odd streetlight that was still in working order lit the warehouses that were no longer in use. This part of the city was perfect for the underground boxing matches. Posh cars rolled through here only on these nights. Homeless people formed dark shadows in the windows of a few buildings apart from the one set up for the boxing. That building had more security than most banks. Rumor had it that a local crime lord ran the ring. I tried not to think about it. The place was a way for me to let off steam and make money for our troupe.

As Travelers, it was difficult to form long-term employment, although many of us had learned a lot of skills over the years. Once we moved on, we couldn't claim all of them. Especially nowadays when the more lucrative jobs required a university education with degrees and the papers to prove it. We were lucky Hamish had gained the skills to make fake identification for us all.

The buildings disappeared from our view and the long expanse of the dark road to our campsite stretched ahead of us.

I turned to Hamish. "Start making the documentation."

He nodded. His mouth pulled down at the edges and his eyes were glum, even in the dark interior, only lit by the lights on the dashboard as he concentrated on the winding road.

Erin sucked in a deep breath from behind me, but she knew better than to argue. She understood our precarious situation. If only we could go back to the way things were before the Trappers.

Life had been so much better back then for the humans and the Fae. Even though I'd been an Earth-born Fae, I'd always known the Summer Court was our true home. The one place we could go. Now we couldn't. I often wondered if I'd visited the Summer Court would I have met the Fae Princess who was my mate sooner? Would I have been with her on that dreadful night? Prevented her injuries?

Would we have had a chance to experience happiness together?

After centuries, I should have stopped thinking about her. Her luminous blue eyes with the indigo ring. Her long lustrous hair hanging at her waist in a thick braid that I'd longed to wind around my wrist and see if she'd enjoy me tugging on it. Enjoy me kissing her plush pink lips. Those thoughts kept me going more than anything.

Hamish swung the car down a dirt road through the gloomy depths of a dark forest. The car bounced along the track and ground to a halt in front of the green and red caravans. Not the type humans purchased these days. Ours were the ones we'd used since we'd been stuck here, changed over the years, but the exterior was the same: curved, colored roof and wagon wheels. Horses still pulled most. They suited our nomadic lifestyle, and our unusual homes kept humans away from us. Except for the real Travelers, when they happened across us, they'd pull up their modern caravans and we'd spend a few days together enjoying their company while keeping our secret since we were Fae. It was difficult to maintain hiding our powers for too long, but they were such pleasant people that we waited, patiently sharing food and stories, warmth and comradeship until they moved onto their next camp. Our lifestyle joined us together. They always left, never knowing we were Fae and while upgrading our abodes to more modern caravans would help us blend in better, we couldn't let go of our past when we'd fought so hard to make it on our own.

Erin exited the car, slamming the door behind her.

"I'll talk to her while you get cleaned up," Hamish said.

"Thanks."

She merged with the troupe of Fae hanging around the campfire. Hamish trudged after her. I trusted him to talk some sense into Erin. He had a calm, fatherly presence that I'd never mastered, even though the troupe regarded me as their leader. I barely knew what

I was doing, but I'd kept us going this long, so I must be doing something right.

I turned and walked through the horses, dozing for the night by the side of the lake. Stripping my clothes, I stepped into the frigid water until I was up to my shoulders. I dunked my head and scrubbed my face under the dark depths of the water. It was icy cold, but as Fae didn't suffer from the cold, it didn't bother me. I might stay here all night, instead of dealing with all the preparations for our upcoming departure from England.

It was time we headed back to our homeland, Ireland. Time we reconnected with the fountain that soothed our powers, because if we didn't go soon, then I wasn't sure what would happen.

# CHAPTER THREE
# AISLINN

I'D FINISHED PACKING A few of my dresses into a travel case when Grier knocked on my chamber door and announced dinner was to be served soon. He'd taken my case in his hand and marched away on his own personal mission. I followed the familiar path to the dining hall. Everyone in the family was in the room when I entered. The conversation stopped and every set of eyes stared at me. My gaze snapped to Briana and the newcomer. He was a large man. Muscular in stature. His arm muscles bulged under the tight confines of his plain white t-shirt. Dark hair and a gaze that assessed everyone and every movement. He watched with the eyes of an alpha wolf. The eyes of a leader taking stock.

"You must be Briana's mate." I stepped around the table.

Briana and her mate stood in a fluid motion of synchronicity that spoke of the depth of their feelings for each other. Her power flared in her palms as though she were about to protect him from me.

I held out my hand.

"Sledge," the large man said, pumping my hand hard. "You're the knife thrower. Briana's memories of your skills were fun to watch. Will you teach me?"

My eyebrows rose. "You want a Fae to teach you?"

"Yeah. Briana taught me her staff, and Saoirse taught me how to sword fight. Knife throwing will be a handy skill to have."

"It is." I smiled.

Her mate was nothing like I'd expected. I slid a knife free from one of the many holsters on my body through the carefully constructed slits in my clothes and lifted the blade under his chin before he realized what I'd done.

"Impressive," he whispered, so his throat didn't shift too much against the blade.

"Aislinn," Mother said. "Put the knives away at the dinner table."

I flicked the blade around and sheathed it, then slid out the chair beside Briana's and sank into the seat.

Sledge held Briana's chair, waited for her to sit, then sat on the other side of her. He leaned closer, as though he couldn't stand to be separated from her.

"How many people have you stabbed with your knives?"

I kept my face expressionless since I'd stabbed no one intending to kill them. The training was a different matter and sometimes when I trained in combat, I'd accidentally inflicted a wound. I'd never intentionally stabbed my sparing partners to hurt them. Luckily, we were immortal and sustaining such injuries wasn't a hardship, as we'd heal in no time at all.

"None of your business."

Sledge smirked. Catching my gaze, he raised one eyebrow. "I suppose you learned wolf shifters can scent lies."

"I did," I said.

"So who's going to tell me why everyone has a crown except Arrow and me?" He gave his mate an amused smile.

"Only males born as Fae Princes will bear a crown," Father said.

"But the women have their pretty flower crowns," Sledge said.

"Aye, they are an extension of our royal powers. Only the males possess the full powers to bestow a Fae crown on their mates."

"Seems sexist," Sledge said.

I hid my grin behind a bread roll. I'd often believed the same thing about the differences in our powers.

"'Tis the way of the Fae." Father shrugged.

"I suppose it's a good thing," Sledge said.

"How so?" Briana asked.

"Could you imagine a wolf running around with a crown of thorns?" he asked.

The entire table burst into laughter. Saoirse's baby gurgled and Rian's mate Sophia stopped laughing as her eyes widened.

"What did he say?" Saoirse asked.

Sophia was a jaguar shifter, and they were telepathic with their kind, but she'd also admitted she could hear the thoughts of all shifters young. It was a handy skill, and I wondered for how long she'd hear the young prince's thoughts.

"He said we'll find out one day."

We all stared at the baby. He was the first of his kind. A Fae royal and a wolf shifter.

"Well," Mother said, patting the flowers of her crown, at a loss for words.

Father's brows pulled together as he tilted his head to the side and studied the baby sitting in his specially made highchair beside Saoirse. As Ailbhe leaned forward, a burst of vines flared from Father's powers and snagged his shoulders, keeping him in place in the twirled mass of the seat. His bottom lip wobbled as though he was about to cry, but an orange butterfly fluttered through the open window and landed on his nose. The baby became cross-eyed and then giggled.

Crisis averted.

We passed plates around the table and soon, with the help of delicious food, conversation flowed between the family. I eyed each of my siblings' mates, surprised at how they were all different, yet they fit in. Fit each of my brothers and sisters like a dream. My two youngest sisters Ciara and Roisin didn't have mates yet, but with the way everyone was finding their fated mate, it wouldn't surprise me if they found theirs soon.

A pity I'd never have mine.

Hours later, we stood at the entrance to the Veil inside the tower Father had made special for a contained doorway between the two realms. A place where he could give us a small amount of freedom while still protecting everyone inside the Summer Court. Rian and Sophia were heading back to the Amazon jungle where Sophia was the jaguar shifter queen ruling over a colony of rare jaguar shifters. Saoirse, Arrow, and Ailbhe were heading back to Crystal Creek with Briana and Sledge, where Sledge was the alpha of a wolf shifter town. Lorcan and Pepper were accompanying me to England, where Pepper had a home. She was the last person I wanted to travel through the Veil with, but Mother was right. This was Lorcan's mate and if he trusted her, then that should be good enough for me. Plus, I didn't know the area. At least Pepper was from England. There were a pair of guards waiting to accompany each royal, as per

Father's orders. The guards had fought in battle where I hadn't. They had the most experience with defending Fae, so I couldn't begrudge the King's order.

One guard stepped forward and said, "Princess Aislinn, I'm Brogan, and this is my brother, Conlan. We'll be your guards on this trip."

I nodded my head at the men who might have been twins with very similar reddish blond hair and pale blue eyes. They both had swords strapped to their backs, as though they were ready to walk into another battle. They'd already fought in the battle of the Trappers. I was safer with them by my side because as much as I didn't admit it to anyone, the night the Trappers had burned me at the stake had scared me.

Rian and Sophia said their goodbyes and left with their guards. The others left not long after, heading back to the wolf shifter community.

Lorcan stepped up to my side. "Ready?"

"Aye."

Whatever was waiting for me in England, I'd find out soon. To say I was excited and nervous was an understatement, but I hid those emotions behind the wall of anger I'd built to hide behind for centuries. Brogan hoisted my travel case into his hand, while his brother, Conlan, carried a much smaller case. I hugged Ciara. Her bottom lip wobbled.

"I'll be back."

Roisin slung her arm around Ciara's waist. "We'll see you soon, Aislinn."

I patted Roisin on the head. She scowled and ducked, but I'd already dropped my hand.

"Next time you do that, I'll use one of your daggers on you."

I laughed. "You think you'll be quick enough?"

"I'll practice while you're away."

"Even more reason for me to come back and see if my training has worked."

Ciara grinned. "I should join these training sessions."

"Girls," Mother reprimanded us. "Your powers are supposed to be used for good."

"We're not using our powers when throwing knives," I pointed out.

Mother huffed.

Father slid his arm around her shoulder but grinned at us over the top of her head. He liked that we could protect ourselves. He'd encouraged us even more after the Trappers to learn how to fight. How to escape. No one would ever tie me to a stake and set me on fire ever again.

"Time to go," Lorcan said. Clasping Pepper's hand in his, he stepped toward the tower.

I followed them with my guards in tow. We all waited for Lorcan to access the Veil before stepping into the glowing blue-green mist. Magic surrounded us. Pulsed against my skin. This was my first time going through the doorway of the Veil. It almost reminded me of the way it felt in the olden days. Almost, but not quite. The magic acted stifled as though it longed to be free once more.

We all had felt that way of late.

A utopia was only paradise if they did not trap you there. Now we were no longer stuck in the Summer Court and traveling to Earth was possible, the mood inside the Fae Kingdom had lifted. More than ever with the news of fated mates being found. All being well, more Fae births would occur now, too.

And with a bit of luck, we'd find a cure for the spring before anyone else realized we were on the cusp of losing our immortality.

The Veil parted, and we stepped out of the magical mist into a weeping willow forest. A cool breeze blew through the leaves, making them brush over my shoulders and hair like the tips of fingers stroking my body. A shiver danced down my spine at the eerie sensation. Beside us, a gentle brook babbled. Birds chirped from the tops of the trees. The place smelled like nature. Lorcan and Pepper walked along the dirt track, willow trees on one side, the water on the other. We followed them, no one saying anything as the path ended in a grassy clearing and a cottage came into view. The dark thatched roof of the house rose into the gloomy gray sky. The clouds hung heavy, appearing like it would rain soon, and the cottage was small.

"Where is everyone staying?" I asked, since there were seven of us on this trip. Two guards for each traveling Fae royal. The protection seemed excessive to me since we had the power to protect ourselves too.

Lorcan frowned at the guards. "Shite, I was in too much of a hurry to get Pepper back to her home that I didn't even think about where everyone would sleep."

Pepper cackled the way witches do. "There is a group of Travelers near here that we might borrow a caravan from. We can park it beside the cottage for the guards to sleep in."

"Good idea," Lorcan said. "Let's put the bags inside, then you can take us to meet them."

"Those guards will have to leave their swords."

The four guards shook their heads.

"Sorry," Lorcan said. "But Pepper is right. Humans don't walk around with swords strapped to their backs these days. We need to blend in and not raise questions about who we are and what we're doing here. The swords will have to stay here."

"But—" Conan said.

"We have our powers, and we have a powerful witch to aid us," Lorcan said. "We'll be able to protect ourselves against humans."

"Damn straight," Pepper said. "Humans have no chance against my potions."

And there lay my problem with Lorcan's mate. She was powerful in a way that could incapacitate any creature.

Including us.

# CHAPTER FOUR
# FALLON

From the water of the lake, I watched my family and friends talking around the campfire. They were so at ease. At home in this countryside. But my mind whirled with the knowledge our wounds weren't healing as fast. What would they say if they knew? Should I tell them?

As the thoughts and indecision warred in my head, I spied the shadowy images of strangers walking toward our secluded camp. They were almost like a mirage. A woman came into clearer view. Long, dark dress. Pale blonde hair. Flowers dotted around her crown. My heart pounded. I blinked my eyes expecting her to disappear, but she was still there. Had my dream come true? All the years of wishing. Wanting and longing to see her even for one moment in time.

My mate.

She was a vision under the beams of the moon as she strode through the forest as though made from the very earthy essence of the place. Her long dress swirled around her legs, tangling with her ankles and revealing her bare feet. With a great effort, I dragged my eyes away from her to take in those walking beside her. A Fae Prince with a crown of thorns. Her brother I assumed. Beside him was a beautiful woman in a long dark cloak. Her beauty did nothing for me. It was my fated mate that my gaze snapped back to. I couldn't believe my eyes.

The cloaked woman stepped in front of my mate revealing the telltale signs of a witch. I narrowed my gaze. What were they doing working with one of her kind? Everyone comprehended they were the reason the Trappers had captured us. A surge of fury burned in my chest. My powers rose making the water spark with a silvery blue electricity as though lightning struck under the water.

The group witnessed the dazzling display of my uncontrolled powers. They stopped walking in an instant. The Fae behind the royals surged in front of them as their powers surged to their hands. Guards. King's guards no less by the red clothes they wore. I strode from the lake as my power crackled from my hands sizzling the water into a stream of steam.

"What are you doing here?" I demanded. All thoughts of my mate had disappeared the instant my rage had taken over my powers.

"You!" My mate screeched.

She shoved past the guards. "Stand down, I know him."

"You do?" the Fae Prince asked.

"Aye," my stunning mate said.

My gaze snapped to my mate's face and drank in the conflicting emotions swirling in her gorgeous eyes. The tight pull of her lips that I longed to plunder in a passionate kiss. The sharp rise and fall of her chest where my power surged to mark her as my mate. She stepped toward me. She was like the vision I'd dreamed of for so long. This moment of finding her. Claiming her became my most insistent urge. My breath stuck in my lungs. Breathing was impossible in her presence for she took my breath away. My power dropped in a sudden rush of longing to hold her in my arms. Closer she stepped. The tension in the air between us was so strong it almost crackled. She was so close I almost reached out to touch her, but my arms had frozen by my sides. Did I dare believe this was real?

Had I fallen asleep in the lake? Imagined her coming to me after all these years. Those dreams never left me. They were what kept me going through the long, isolated days and nights.

A sharp sting flared in my chest. I glared down. The hilt of a blade protruded from my chest. Agony impaled my heart.

My lips parted in shock. "You stabbed me."

"Aye," she said. "Now you understand what it feels like."

I gasped as my lungs shot back to life. The pain almost dropped me to my knees on the ground before her feet.

"I don't understand."

She lifted another blade. "Do I need to stab you again to make it clear?"

"Perhaps." I studied the glint of anger in her eyes. And here I believed she'd been as overwhelmed with gratitude as I was at seeing my mate again. No dream I'd ever imagined had resulted in her stabbing me in the heart.

She forced the tip of the blade into the skin on my chest, but it was nothing compared to the pain from the dagger already imbedded in my heart. It was fortunate a blade to the heart couldn't kill Fae otherwise I'd be dead. By the hands of my fated mate no less.

"You left me," she said through gritted teeth. "Now you can suffer the agony I've experienced for centuries."

I grabbed her wrist holding the knife and dragged her into my body, only then remembering I was naked from my dip in the lake. But every inch of her luscious body against me commanded mine to life with lust even through the smarting in my chest.

"Are you for real?" She tilted her head back.

"You're real. You're here." I slammed my lips against hers, the desire for my mate too much to deny. The improbability of this ever occurring urged me to take what I'd let go all those years ago when I should have hung onto her forever.

A sharp pain exploded along my lip. I reared my head back, touching the tender flesh. My mate bit me. She took my moment of shock to slam her head into my nose. Blood burst as bone crunched. She spun out of my arms and kicked me in the face. I flew backward, landing on the ground with an inelegant grunt of discomfort.

The second time tonight someone had beaten me down.

"What the Dia, Aislinn?" a masculine voice asked.

Her brother? Was that my mate's name?

"Aislinn?" I groaned her name.

I yanked the dagger from my chest and sat up. The guards surrounded me and so did her brother. Their power flared from their hands in dazzling displays. My power surged at the perceived threat standing over me. Shouts and hollers rang out behind us. Thundering footsteps exploded across the ground. I jumped to my feet as the skin over my heart knitted itself back together but inside the organ was still repairing itself. My mother had always told me that if anyone mortally wound a Fae the Spring of Life would heal them. If I could access the spring in the Summer Court, I'd heal in an instant. As it was, my mate had weakened me for a day or two until I healed completely.

Hamish arrived at my side first, his hands glowing an unearthly red. The rest of our troupe ground to a halt beside him.

The tension that shouldn't have been between us all was like a live current.

"Who are you all?" Hamish asked since I couldn't seem to form a word after finding my mate.

After being stabbed by her. Not exactly the way I'd imagined we'd meet again.

"I'm Prince Lorcan, this is my mate, Pepper. Our guards, Patrick, Declan, Brogan, and Conlan. My sister Princess Aislinn, it appears, is fated to him." The Fae Prince nodded his crowned head toward me. "They know each other."

"We met once," I rasped out.

"You snatched me away from my brother as he was rescuing me! Carried me away like an invalid, and yes I know the fire burned my feet, but you didn't give me a choice."

"I knew you were my mate, and I had to save you."

"Save me?" She snorted. "Lorcan already saved me. All you did was call me your mate."

"You are my mate and I'm yours."

"Then why did you leave me?" she asked with a hitch in her breath at the end.

"I had to. You don't understand. I didn't have time to explain or even ask which princess you were."

"You'd think a mate would have time to ask his mate her name," Aislinn said with enough heat in her words to char the entire forest.

She told the truth, but I hadn't the time that night to learn her name.

"I know it now." My lips stretched into a smile of their own accord. Her name would fall from my lips every day from here on. "Aislinn. My fated mate."

Her eyes narrowed. "You are no mate of mine."

I flinched worse than when she'd stabbed me with her dagger. The words hurt more than the blade too.

"I'm yours and you are mine. That's the way it is."

She opened her mouth, but her brother stepped in front of her.

"How about you get dressed and we can talk like civilized Fae over food and drink?"

I'd forgotten about my nakedness with the shock of the moment. I stepped back toward the lake where I'd left my clothes, not once taking my eyes from the half-hidden shape of my mate behind the guards. Her brother whispered into her ear, and she shook her head. He grinned back at her as though he found the entire moment amusing. I dressed fast and rushed back to them.

Hamish slapped me on the back. "Follow us. We have a lot of questions, like how are you here on Earth?"

We led the way back to the campfire, our troupe settled on one side of the glowing orange flames, while the newcomers stayed on the other side.

"A short time ago the King created a doorway in the locked Veil," Prince Lorcan said.

I hadn't sensed it. I suppose I hadn't tried breaching the locked Veil for years. If I hadn't given up, then I would have found the doorway and my mate sooner.

"We only now heard about Fae still being on Earth and as soon as we learned there were Fae trapped on Earth, we searched for you," he said.

My eyes narrowed. "You didn't stop to think some of us didn't make it through the Veil before the King locked it all those years ago?"

The Prince ran his gaze over the troupe. "We assumed the Trappers killed any Fae left here before we annihilated them all."

"Bit presumptuous to think we hadn't avoided them."

"No." Aislinn almost yelled the word. "They sent word out to all the Fae settlements on the day of the massacre. They warned every Fae who was still alive. Every Fae was told they'd be safe in the Summer Court. It takes a mere moment to access the Veil. If you didn't make it through the Veil in time, then that's on you."

Oh, my mate appeared furious, but so was I. Her father had kept me from her for centuries.

Hamish coughed dramatically and passed around mugs of lager. The Summer Court Fae accepted his offering while my mate kept the daggers in her eyes aimed at me. They were as sharp as the blades she'd stabbed me with.

"Sorry to say, I didn't make it through in time, the same as everyone here, because a group of children was hiding from the Trappers, and we had to find them."

My mate's face whitened. She lowered herself to the nearest log placed around the campfire.

"My sister was one of those hiding," I said, driving home the point.

She exchanged a glance with her brother. It appeared she understood the bond between siblings.

Maybe she'd forgive me for not putting her first that night.

Perhaps one day I'd forgive myself.

# CHAPTER FIVE
## AISLINN

HAD HIS WORDS ELIMINATED my anger? No. But they had lessened the resentment running through my veins in the heat of my blood. I sipped the mug in my hands. A bitter taste hit my tongue. I spluttered the liquid onto the ground. My mate laughed. So did the rest of the Earth-dwelling Fae. Fae who we'd trapped on Earth. While the King had sealed us inside the Summer Court, we had left them to experience life without access to the Fae Kingdom. Sorrow built in my chest and tears welled in my eyes. I blinked them away. My mate's laughter died.

A second later he kneeled in front of me, removed the mug from my hands and clasped my palms in his.

"Aislinn." He sighed my name like he couldn't stop saying it.

I lifted my gaze to his face. He was the most gorgeous man I'd ever laid eyes on. I'd dreamed of his face. The vibrant light blue of his eyes and the way his dark brows made them even more magical. My fingers itched to stroke the soft fall of his dark hair over the sides of his forehead. Today he had a layer of stubble on his face. A bruise was forming around one eye and his nose appeared crooked. I longed to reach out and straighten it, but our immortality would fix his broken bones. Soft pink lips parted as his tongue darted out and licked them. Every ounce of my being demanded I kiss him.

He'd kissed me before, and I'd been too angry, too full of rage to respond to his advance except to cause him pain. The agony of him leaving me when he understood what we meant to each other was still there. I'd probably never get over it.

"What's your name?" I asked, forgetting everyone in the camp.

"Fallon," he said in his accented voice. "Fallon O'Sullivan."

His thumbs stroked the soft, sensitive skin on my wrists.

"You're more beautiful than I remember."

"Considering ash and burns covered me at the time I should hope so."

His thick brows dipped into a frown. "You were beautiful even then."

"I assumed you died," I said around the lump forming in my throat.

All these years, I'd believed I'd met my fated mate, he'd forsaken me for others and had died before we'd even known each other. Before, we'd loved each other as fated mates.

"If I'd known you were alive, I would have searched all the realms for you."

I released one hand and cupped her cheek. "I tried for many years to breech the locked Veil."

"It would have been pointless." I shook my head imagining him trying and failing to go through the locked Veil. "Only royal powers can breech the lock."

"You. You were able to come here?"

"Aye, my siblings and I have royal powers. We snuck here when possible because—" I trailed off. I couldn't tell them about the spring. No one knew but the royal family. "I never sensed you."

"Do you sense me now?" He placed my hand on his chest.

My power surged with the need to mark my mate. I snatched my hand away before the power overwhelmed me. If I marked him and him me, then we'd fall into the Quiet to absorb each other's memories, but I didn't want to do that on Earth. I wanted the safety of the Summer Court, and the chance to talk to Fallon about the failing Spring of Life in private.

"I do."

"Then let's not waste any more time apart. Mark me."

I drew my other hand from his. "Now is not the time. Father tasked us with fetching you home to the Summer Court."

I'd always intended to search for a solution to our Spring of Life while here. I'd never imagined we'd find the Fae so quickly. It was almost too easy as though fate had a hand in it. Was Saltine's vision right? Had she sent me here at this time to find my fated mate?

He rocked back on his heels. "I'm afraid I can't go there yet."

"Why?" I asked.

"Because I'm mad. The King locked the Veil and kept me from you."

"Oh," I whispered. "He didn't know. I told no one I'd met you that night. I believed the Trappers had killed you."

"Aye, thanks for that," Lorcan said. "I knew something had happened that night, yet you kept telling me nothing had."

"The pain was mine to bear. I believed my fated mate had died."

Lorcan placed an arm around my shoulders. "We'll talk."

I nodded. Now he understood everything I'd kept hidden all these years, it would be a relief to voice it to my brother.

"So now the King wants us?" another Fae asked.

"He always wanted to protect every Fae," Lorcan said. "If he'd known you were here, he would have searched for you all sooner."

"Hamish," Fallon said. "Our anger might be unwarranted, but it will take us time to move past it. You can't expect us to let it go in one minute because you say otherwise."

"I don't," I said. "Because I won't. You can't expect me to move on from my resentment that you left me that night and didn't return to the Summer Court with me."

"Aislinn." He groaned my name.

"We came here to ask to borrow a caravan for our guards to sleep in," Lorcan said.

"A caravan?" Fallon's brow puckered. "Take what you need. You're my mate, but I'd prefer you to stay here near me."

"I can't." I shook my head, my thick braid swished so hard it slapped my back.

"Very well." He clicked his fingers. "Hamish, hook up a horse to a caravan and give them what they need."

Hamish scowled and grumbled under his breath, but he stood and walked toward the herd of dozing horses.

"But mate, you're mistaken if you think I'd let you out of my sight." Fallon stood. "Wherever you go. I go too."

There were the words I'd wanted to hear all those centuries ago, and now, they didn't have quite the same meaning as they would have back then. My heart wasn't in it. All Fae longed for their fated mate. Wished for them. And here was mine right in front of me, yet I was reluctant to grasp the happiness we'd share.

I stood, and so did my guards. I inched away from Fallon, away from my chance at experiencing happiness.

"You can't forsake me," he said, standing too.

"Why not?" I asked. "You did it to me."

# CHAPTER SIX
# FALLON

I SHIFTED BEFORE CONSCIOUS thought and grabbed for my mate. The guards closed ranks around her, halting my progress.

"Stand down," Prince Lorcan said. "Her mate would never hurt her."

"He already did," Aislinn said and rushed into the forest.

Her brother sighed. "Best you go after her. And watch out for her daggers."

Yeah, there were those to keep in mind. I didn't want to get stabbed in the heart again. The organ still throbbed from the sting of her wound, but it was her words that hurt me more. I dashed through the forest, drawn by the sweet scent of my mate. She smelled like the first fresh breeze of spring with the perfumed scent of fresh-budded wildflowers. My legs and arms pumped in time for my hurried run. I caught up with Aislinn. She spun, throwing a dagger at my chest, but I dodged to the side a fraction too fast for her blade to hit me.

Damn, she was feisty, and it was making me want her even more.

"You can stab me all you like if that's what will make you happy."

She stopped and twirled another blade in her hand. The moonlight glinted off the Fae material. So magical that I'd forgotten how much power we Fae possessed in our bodies and the Fae Kingdom.

"But you don't want to hurt me."

"I don't?"

She appeared so confused. The front she put on, the hard exterior and anger that fueled the throw of her knives wobbled. I'd break through those walls and show her how much she meant to me. She'd never doubt that ever again.

"No." I inched closer to Aislinn. "You want me to want you."

Her bottom lip quivered.

"You want me to love you."

The quiver turned into a tremble.

"Let me be the mate you deserved."

She tossed her head from side to side. "You don't want me."

"I do."

"You didn't."

"I did even back then. It was the worst decision of my life letting you go back to the Summer Court without me. I should have kept you by my side, but I couldn't do it, not after seeing you injured. Not knowing there were Trappers still hunting us." I drew in a calming breath as the anguish of that night returned to me tenfold. "Not knowing I might lose you when I'd just found you. I needed you safe. Alive. I recognized you'd be safe in the Summer Court. And you were, weren't you?"

"I was safe," she whispered.

"Believe me when I say I regret my choice. I regret losing all those years with you."

Tears fell from her lashes onto her cheeks.

I inched closer still to Aislinn as her body shook. The blade wobbled in her hand, and I gently placed my palm over the hilt and pointed it toward the ground. It fell from her tight grip to the ground thudding faintly on the forest floor. Above us, an owl hooted, and its white wings flashed through the branches.

"Regrets are hard to live with," I said, ever so gradually sliding my other hand around her waist. "I've played that night over in my head so many times wondering how I would have changed it. How I would have saved my sister as well as kept you by my side. I want you by my side forever."

I slid my arm up her back reveling in the shivers running over her body at my touch. My palm met her soft skin, and my thumb brushed the damp tears from her cheeks. More fell to take their place.

"Please stop crying."

"Why?" she whispered.

"Because your tears hurt me more than your dagger to my heart."

A tiny smile tipped the corners of her deep pink lips. Lips I hungered to kiss. To place my claim on her body in any way she'd let me. To make her see how much she meant to me without words but with the language of our bodies.

"You hurt me," she hissed. "For so very long. You chose another over your mate."

"My sister was a toddler hiding from our enemy. Would you have been able to live with her death on our hands if we'd left?"

"No, I would have done the same for any of my siblings."

A small amount of hope surged in my chest. I lowered my head toward hers unable to stop myself from kissing her. She didn't stab me or stop me in any other way. Her lips parted. Softly I placed mine on hers. The connection was instantaneous. She was my destiny. The one made for me. I swiped my tongue over her lips tasting the saltiness of her tears. I hated that I'd made her cry. Hated that I'd made her sad. I despised myself for not putting her first. She would be first from this moment forward. No one and nothing would ever get between us again.

Her tongue touched mine tentatively as though she had the same passions and feelings as me that this wasn't real. I needed to prove to both of us that it was. There was nothing more real than the connection of fated mates. I slid one hand to the back of her head, cradling the thick braid against her scalp in a tight hold. My nerve endings burst to life in my palm. I held her head close to mine giving her no chance to break the kiss or put distance between us once more. There would never be distance ever again.

She melted into my hold as though she needed my firm hand. The pressure of holding her in place so she didn't flee from the depth of emotions sparking to life between us. I trailed my other hand down her back over her hip and drew her lower body against mine. A shiver ran through her body as she experienced the evidence of how much I wanted her. Needed her. The hardness of my erection surprised even me. I'd never once been with another woman. Even considered another woman when I knew the King had locked my fated mate away in the Summer Court and here she was in my arms. She kissed me with the same passion that was overwhelming me.

It obliterated every thought of the past from my mind. There was only here and now. The curve of her body against mine. Tiny gasps of pleasure came from deep in her throat as our tongues twined in a kiss that would never end. I didn't want it to end. The desire to never let her go kept my lips on hers. I'd kiss her forever and a day and it still wouldn't be enough. Dreams of her lips haunted my life before today. I'd never get enough of my mate.

I lightened the kiss enough to say, "Stay with me here tonight, please."

Then I was back kissing her again with the unparalleled passion only a mate invoked. She sighed and rubbed against my body as though she was as hungry for me as I was for her. I wanted to lay her out on my mattress and worship her body. She was a princess and deserved more than the dirt of the forest floor.

"Please, Aislinn?"

"Aye," she said so quietly I almost didn't hear it.

I scooped up her fallen dagger and handed it back to Aislinn. She offered me a small smile that warmed the ache in my heart at losing her. Gathering her hand in mine, I walked with her back to the camp. Her brother, his mate, and the guards were still there sitting around the fire talking to my troupe. The group of Fae were mine. They'd been mine since we'd joined after that dreadful night. We'd come together in the depths of our despair and sadness and formed an unbreakable connection.

"Everything all right?" Prince Lorcan asked his sister.

"We're working on it," Aislinn said.

"The wagon is ready," Hamish said, striding back into the camp. "It sleeps two."

"Perfect," the prince said. "We'll head back now and get some rest. Tomorrow we'll come back and talk to you again about visiting the Summer Court."

"Okay," I said, because if my mate lived in the Summer Court then I'd have to visit the damn place one day. It would be best to rip the bandage off my hurt sooner rather than later. Wounds festered like regret.

"I'm staying here," Aislinn said surprising me she didn't go back on her agreement.

The prince and the guards didn't look happy, but they all yielded to the princess even though two of the guards stayed behind. I guess we had to offer another caravan for them to sleep in. By chance, we traveled with a few extra caravans for storing goods in, but since we'd been here so long and had built a rapport with the local village, we hadn't the need to store such large amounts the last few years.

"Everyone get some rest," I said to the troupe. "We have a lot to discuss tomorrow."

Murmurs rippled through the gathered group of Fae as they wandered off to their caravans. I walked toward my caravan with the bright blue roof shining under the moonlight and the painted gold figures on the doorway glowing with what many rumored as magic. No matter how careful we were humans believed Travelers were magic. We couldn't discount the claim, so we tried our best to quell the rumors of magical powers. Rumors were just that though. Regular Travelers didn't possess magical powers. We'd met enough over the years to learn of their heritage, and they'd not come from any supernatural beings. They were regular humans. Friendly too. We enjoyed their ways even though we weren't like them. Even less so now in modern times.

"Is this yours?" Aislinn asked.

"Yes. I've upgraded it over the years, but it's been with me for a long time."

"Your home is here?"

"In this caravan, yes. Here in England, no. We travel every few years so humans don't question how we don't age."

"Smart," she said. "This is Brogan and Conlan my guards while I'm here."

"Has the King learned of a threat here?"

"No. He's paranoid. Cautious and overbearing with his protection. He blames himself for what happened with the Trappers. It's why he took the King's guards to wipe out every last one of them."

I observed her climb the steps to the caravan door. I'd learned the tales of the King's massacre in retaliation for the Trappers afterward, but I'd been searching for Erin and the other children at the time otherwise I would have offered my services to help him.

"Do you two need to check inside is safe before the princess enters?" I asked.

One of them stepped forward and climbed the steps beside my mate. The closeness of his body next to hers made me want to tear him away and throw him across the camp. I curled my fingers into my palms and willed my power not to surge otherwise I'd send a bolt of electricity through them and who knows what powers they possessed that they'd use in retaliation. I wouldn't risk Aislinn being hurt in the crossfire.

"Stay here while I check," the guard said.

Aislinn folded her arms and rolled her eyes at me. I almost laughed at her sass, but the guards were for her protection, and I'd do anything to keep her safe even if it meant I had to wait a few more minutes until I'd have her alone and to myself.

The guard slipped through the door and disappeared into the caravan. He wouldn't find anything malicious there.

He returned a few minutes later and nodded at me before descending the steps. I walked up to my mate. She dropped her folded arms, and her face lit with interest as though she was excited to see inside my home. I opened the door for Aislinn. She swept inside, her purple dress swishing around her legs. I'd forgotten the way Fae material was so light and airy. So magical like her. Her soft gasp of delight made me rush inside and close the door behind us sealing us in the cozy interior of my caravan.

"Do you like it?"

# CHAPTER SEVEN
## AISLINN

WHAT WASN'T TO LIKE? The interior of the wooden caravan was way more luxurious than I imagined. Deep red curtains hung from the window at the end overhanging the sumptuous-looking bed with an array of red cushions and the occasional blue one thrown in for contrast. The blanket appeared to have intricate stitching of vines and leaves with yellow sunflowers sewn in the mixture. I dragged my gaze away from the bed because staring at the inviting mattress, all I thought about was having my mate in bed with me.

He'd lined one wall with cupboards top and bottom with a space in between for a set of pale blue teacups.

They didn't seem masculine enough for Fallon, and the entire interior of the caravan seemed more feminine than masculine. Was he with another woman? Had he chosen a mate instead of waiting for me?

I sat on the small bench seat on the opposite wall as my knees gave way to the anguish those ideas produced in my heart. He understood I was alive, so it wasn't as if he couldn't have waited for me.

"You don't like it," he said.

"It's very feminine," I said tucking my hands under my thighs so I wouldn't stab him again. "The woman who decorated it must be..."

I couldn't even say anything nice about the woman who was with my mate.

"She's a pain in my ass," he grumbled.

My head jerked his way as surprise rolled through me that he said such a thing about the woman he'd chosen to be his mate.

"Why choose her then?"

He rubbed a hand over his chest. "I keep telling you I regret choosing my sister."

Frowning, I said, "I'm so confused. I meant the woman you chose as your mate."

"What?" he spluttered.

I waved my hand around the inside of the caravan. "A woman decorated this, no?"

His eyebrows rose. "No. I mean yes. My sister decorated the caravan. She's decorated all of them. It's what she does."

"Your sister?" I asked, incredulous.

He smirked. "You were jealous."

"I was not." I folded my arms over my chest before I stabbed him again.

"You were, and it was cute." He stepped toward the teacups. "I would never choose another."

He poured a jug of brown liquid into two teacups and carried them toward me. Settling on the small seat beside me, he held one teacup out.

"Sweet tea," he said.

"I'm not sure." I wrinkled my nose recalling the taste of the lager.

"Try it. You might like it."

I uncrossed my arms and accepted the teacup. Staring at the floating pieces of lemon, I couldn't stop the sensations running through my body with Fallon so close to me. His scent was strong this close and each minute we spent inside the caravan made it even stronger until my head swam with the aroma of cedarwood and spices. He sipped his cup and surveyed me over the rim. I couldn't tear my gaze away from the way his lips caressed the lip of the cup. Dia, his kisses had been so delightful. Heat worked its way across my cheeks.

Fallon lowered the cup. "Why are you blushing? I didn't peg you as the type to blush."

"Am I?" I raised my free hand to my warm cheek. "It must be hot in here that's all."

"Hot?" He raised a questioning eyebrow.

"Mm-hm." I lifted the teacup to my lips and took a tentative sip.

Sweetness exploded over my tongue with a tang of lemon too. I tipped the cup and drank the rest as it was delicious.

"Did you like it?"

"Aye." I handed him the empty teacup.

"Good. I got something right with my mate." He placed my empty cup and his half-full one on a small wooden table. "We discovered it when we traveled America for a few years and now we make it wherever we go."

"Have you traveled a lot?"

"Yes, but Ireland will always be our home. We head back there more than anywhere else. England is pleasant enough but there's no place like home."

"You were born in Ireland?"

"Yes."

"So were my mother's parents and the rest of her family. I'm surprised we didn't meet sooner because I loved spending time with them. We all did."

Grief hit me like a punch to the stomach. It never ceased to amaze me how hard grief would overcome me even after all this time.

"My entire family died that night. All except Erin."

The sadness in his voice made me look at Fallon and study him. I understood loss, but at least I hadn't lost my parents.

"I'm sorry," I said.

"It wasn't your fault."

"No, it wasn't, but I'm sorry you lost loved ones. I understand how much it hurts."

"It never leaves you, does it?"

I shook my head. My eyes welled with tears again. I blinked them back. I didn't want to cry in his presence again.

Clearing my throat I said, "So what now?"

"That's up to you."

"I need to take you back to the Summer Court."

He sighed.

"My father wants to meet you all."

"Can we discuss something else?"

"Like what?"

"Tell me what your life has been like since you won't allow us to exchange mating marks and our memories yet."

"I imagine a lot different to yours. I live in the Fae palace. I train. I eat. I sleep. Nothing special."

"You are special." His fingers found the heavy end of my braid and tugged the ribbon free. "Can I see your hair down?"

"Whatever for?" I tugged my braid out of his grasp.

"At night, when I was lying here alone dreaming of you, I'd think of your hair, how it had streamed in a silvery blonde halo around your head, and how soft it was under my palm. I longed to stroke my fingers through the strands and touch the living gold."

"That's very poetic." I tried not to smile and failed. "What do you do with your days?"

"I fight."

I took in the bluish hue of a bruise around his eye in the cozily lit interior of the caravan. Now that he'd said that I ran a more critical eye over him. His crooked nose

I'd noted earlier had already straightened, but there were lingering signs of fighting on his body.

"Why?"

He shrugged his muscular shoulders. "It helps me release my fury, so my powers don't overwhelm me. It's been difficult to keep our powers hidden for so long."

"I don't even use my powers anymore."

"What?" He stood so fast the caravan wobbled a tiny fraction. "Why ever not?"

"I mean, I used them a few times to breach the locked Veil—"

He groaned. "You were able to come through the lock a lot?"

"No. I didn't for a long time until it was necessary."

"Why was it necessary?"

"Oh." I peered down at my hands. "The... I... oh."

A slow smile formed on his lips as he patiently waited for me to answer.

What might I tell him? I should tell him everything. Mates shouldn't have secrets, but I found it hard to trust him.

"You don't want to tell me?"

"Not yet."

"I suppose that's fair enough. I don't like it, but I will earn your trust."

"We'll see," I said.

"We will," he agreed. "And when I'm right, will you tell me?"

I laughed. "I doubt it."

"Mate," he said with a growl, "are you trouble?"

# CHAPTER EIGHT
# FALLON

THAT WOULD DEPEND ON your definition of trouble," she replied with all the sass in the world.

Damn, I wanted to bend her over my knee and spank her, but there was time for that later. Besides, she might not enjoy that sort of thing. My cock jumped to attention at the image of her spread across my knees though. I shifted on the seat but ended up brushing my leg against hers and igniting my need for my mate even more. Her breath hitched letting me recognize my closeness affected her as much as her closeness affected me.

"I could stay up all night talking to you, but we should get some sleep."

Her gaze darted to the bed.

"Will you sleep beside me?"

"Sleep?"

Did she sound disappointed?

"Whatever you desire."

She stood and walked a few steps to the bed before sitting on the edge.

"And if I desire more?"

"Then I'd give it to you." I stepped closer until the tips of my toes touched hers.

She peered up at me all doe-eyed with her magical eyes of blue rimmed with indigo. My fingers found the ends of her hair and tugged the ribbon free and unraveled the length of the thick braid. Each pass of my fingers sent a shiver through her.

"If we have sex now, it doesn't mean I'll mark you."

My fingers paused. "It means I'm making love to my mate."

Her chest rose as she drew in a deep breath.

"Let me worship you."

She nodded her head a tad I'd have missed if I hadn't been so absorbed with my mate. My fingers resumed untying her hair, and I took my time reveling in the fact she was here in my bed. As the last knot tumbled free, her tresses fell over her shoulders in the living silk I remembered. I ran my fingers through the strands until a sigh left Aislinn's mouth. She tipped her head forward and my already hard cock had ideas about her mouth on it. I willed that image away because this was about her and showing her how much she meant to me.

I lowered to my knees in front of her and gathered the hem of her long dress in my hands. The Fae material was almost as soft as her hair. I slid the skirt up her calves until it rested on her knees. She had a dagger strapped at her ankle, and it surprised me for a moment. I slid the buckle free and let the sheath and blade fall to the floor. My palms cupped the back of her legs and massaged her bared skin. Even her skin was silkier than anything I dreamed up.

As I lifted her right leg, I glided my hand down to her foot and massaged the sole with enough pressure that Aislinn moaned. The sound sent a shot of desire straight to my cock. I lowered her foot, and she rubbed it against my cock making me moan. She kept her foot there teasing me with it while I picked up her left foot and massaged that one too.

She inched her dress higher up her legs drawing my gaze to the creamy expanse of her bared thighs. Thighs that were covered in more dagger holsters and daggers. I let out a soft chuckle, but she drew the dress higher still until I caught the pretty pink flash of flesh between her legs. Seemed my mate was as greedy for me as I was for her. No matter the issues we still needed to work out, our bodies didn't care about those. I dropped her foot and slid my hands up the curvaceous length of her thighs. When I reached the tip of the blades, I undid the dagger holsters, catching them and placing them on the floor beside the other one. My fingers resumed their caress until they skated over the soft curls to the awaiting heaven between her legs.

I ran my hands up the inside of her floaty dress, pausing I said, "Another one?"

Aislinn laughed as I unbuckled that dagger holster too and placed it with her collection.

"Any more?"

"No," she said, still laughing.

I resumed my caress of her body, cupping her bare breasts and rasping my thumbs over her nipples. A full body shiver wracked her body. I forced down tenderly on her chest urging her to lay back. To let me take care of her. She did, and I inched forward, placing my mouth on the heady aroma of her arousal coming from between her legs. I slicked my tongue over her clit. Her back shot off the bed. I dragged a hand back down her stomach and pinned it to the mattress before sampling her with my tongue again. This time when her back bowed, I was ready to keep her in place. Ready to feast on her like a starving man.

And I was.

All those years without her had famished me.

Starved from loving my mate.

And love her I would.

Right now, I'd love her with my body, and tomorrow, and the next day, I'd love her again. In time, she'd see how much she meant to me. In time, she'd love me too.

I licked and suckled her until her breath fell in stuttering gasps. Until her thighs quivered around my head and I considered she was trying to squeeze the life out of my skull. What a way to go, if I was human, that was, and could die that way.

Raising her legs, I spread her wide and devoured her flesh. She whimpered and moaned. She wriggled to get out of my grasp, but I held her tighter still. Oh, she was trouble with a capital T. But she was perfect. The tremors of her body quietened as every muscle pulled tight like a bow string. Her breathing stopped.

Then suddenly, she came on my tongue. Her breathing resumed as she moaned and thrashed on the bed with the force of the contractions overtaking her body. The force of the pleasure I'd given my mate. And I'd give her more. Every day. Every minute.

Whatever she wanted.

She was mine to love and cherish.

"Fallon," she gasped my name as I kept licking her quivering flesh. "Enough."

I stopped at once. She touched a hand to my head and ran her fingers through the long strands at my forehead. I sighed into her touch placing a gentle kiss on Aislinn's mound before sliding up her body.

"That was... epic."

"Good." I placed my hands under her shoulders and rolled us over until she was lying on my chest.

She sighed and sunk into my embrace. My cock raged against her softness begging me to bury it deep inside her. Claim her. My power surged to my palms, but I kept my focus on my control. The focus to keep it under control. The determination to not give into the overwhelming urge to mark her as my mate. Aislinn's body grew softer. Heavier against mine.

Was she falling asleep?

I suppose that was what I deserved, but I couldn't complain with her taste on my tongue, her moans of pleasure ringing in my ears, and her soft body flattened against mine, if she needed to sleep then I'd let her. I'd wanted the chance to hold her close for so long that if I didn't sleep a wink, then it wouldn't matter. But holding her while stroking her back and silky hair was enough right now.

We had forever together.

Because I'd never let her leave my sight again.

# CHAPTER NINE
## AISLINN

I STRETCHED THEN FROZE. A warm body was curled behind me. A heavy arm hung over my waist and cupped between my legs. Shite. Fallon. I'd fallen asleep in his arms after he'd given me the most amazing orgasm of my life. What a terrible thing to do to him, but I suppose that's why fated mates were so longed for. I couldn't wait to see what sex would be like with him.

Explosive.

Or was that implosive?

Either way, I was hooked.

Hooked on him. The way he made me feel. The way he declared he'd love me forever. Put me first forever.

For so long I'd wanted that and now I had it in my grasp. I lifted my hand and slid it backward cupping the back of his head.

"Good morning," he said huskily.

I snatched my hand back since I assumed he was asleep. He lifted his hand and caught mine, then lifted it to his lips kissing it tenderly.

"Did you sleep well?" he asked.

"I haven't slept that well since… well, you understand. Nightmares plague my sleep. I don't recall having one last night. Did I?"

"You didn't so much as twitch."

I rolled over, my hand sliding to cup his cheek. "Didn't you sleep?"

"No. I couldn't close my eyes long enough to fall asleep. I had to keep checking you were real. Really here."

"I'm here," I whispered.

"But you want to return to the Summer Court."

"I do."

"So I need to shove my rage aside and accompany you."

I rolled my head to the side. "You don't need to do anything."

"I *need* to be with *you*."

A smile tugged at my lips. Perhaps Fallon would win me over sooner than either of us imagined. Or maybe heading back to the Summer Court would destroy the fragile bond we'd formed.

"You can show me this place first."

"Yeah?"

I bit my lip and nodded.

He leaned closer and kissed me with such sweet tenderness another wall around my heart crumbled. Soon they'd be rubble at his feet. He trailed his lips to my cheek, and higher to my forehead where he placed his lips and held them still against me as though placing a different claiming mark on my skin. One that I'd sense every time I thought about it.

Noises outside became louder, the sounds of people moving about, talking, joyous voices. I longed to meet his people in daylight under better circumstances than when I'd just stabbed him. My hand shot to his chest.

"Are you healed yet?"

"Almost."

I dropped my hand and sagged back on the mattress. "I should say I'm sorry for stabbing you."

"But you're not." He smirked.

"No." I sat up and patted all the places I kept my daggers. There wasn't a single dagger on my body or the straps that held them in place but then I remembered the way Fallon had taken them off me while touching me.

"Your daggers are on the floor."

I crawled to the edge of the mattress and peered over the side. My discarded daggers glittered in the early morning sunlight streaming through the small window of the caravan. In the daylight, the place was even more charming. It had such a cozy atmosphere it was easy to see that despite his sister's touch, this place was Fallon's.

The row of cups along the counter under the overhead cupboards said he liked to drink a lot of sweet tea. Perhaps even hot tea. The dark timber of the cabinetry was the most masculine accent in the caravan. On the other side, the bench seat appeared as though made for his size. The bed was the focal point at the end of the caravan perched under the window. The forest outside made the place feel as though we were inside nature instead of a spectator. I gathered my blades and strapped them to my body in the same way I had been doing for many years.

"That is more of a turn-on than I imagined it would be," Fallon said, his voice thick with arousal.

As I lifted my gaze, I found Fallon watching me with a hungry expression. I should feel bad that I'd fallen asleep after he'd given me an orgasm since I'd probably left him aroused. My gaze traveled to his waist and lower, to the thick bulge of his erection throbbing against his pants. Pants he hadn't stripped off.

But in the light of day, I couldn't force myself to close the gap between us. Last night had been different. The shock of finding him alive coupled with my insane attraction for him had left me unable to resist the carnal urges of fated mates. I brushed back the tangled knots of my long hair, softly cursing him for unbraiding it.

"Allow me," he said, grabbing a hairbrush resting on a small shelf above the bed.

Did he want to brush my hair? He inched closer and gathered the thick tresses in one hand, gently separating my hair into a section, he set to work combing the knots from my hair. Every pass of his hands made a tiny shiver dance over my scalp. Each gust of his warm breath on the back of my neck made me bite my lip to stop from moaning. Fallon brushing my hair was more erotic than I imagined. Was it the fact my fated mate was taking care of me that made it seem more? Made me want more too. And when he touched the flowers in my princess crown, my powers surged with the need to mark him as mine.

I stood so swiftly it surprised both of us. Fallon's eyebrows rose as his gaze swept over my body.

"Problem?"

"No." I gathered my hair in my glowing palms, surprised to see the soft purple hue coming from them. "We should..."

"Yes?" He placed the hairbrush back on the shelf and reclined on the bed as though he had all the time in the world.

"Talk to the others. See if everyone will return to the Summer Court and talk to the King."

Fallon groaned. "Way to make my erection go down."

My gaze snapped to his erection. It didn't look like it had decreased one bit since the last time I'd stared at it.

"Liar," I said with a breathy laugh.

"At least I made you laugh." He smirked.

I shook my head. After our rocky meeting. Fallon was unexpectedly different from any Fae I'd met. And I'd met a lot of Earth-living Fae before the King sealed the Veil. My mother's family lived on Earth after all. Or had. I frowned.

"Now you're scowling again. What did I do wrong?"

"Nothing. It wasn't you. Terrible memories popped into my mind." I started braiding my hair to give my hands something to do, otherwise, I'd throw the knives at the nearest target and his caravan was too pretty to be littered with dagger marks on the timber surface. "It's hard to forget."

"They are. It doesn't mean we can't be happy now though. My parents would have wanted me to be happy even after they died."

My fingers stilled in my hair. "You seem remarkably at ease to talk about the loss of your parents."

His lips firmed.

"I find it hard to talk about the ones we lost." My fingers resumed the braiding of my hair. "How do you do it and not suffer crippling sadness?"

"I'm sad."

As I arrived at the end of my braid, I gathered the fallen ribbon and tied it around the ends.

"I suppose I don't know you well enough to say if you're sad or not."

"If we marked each other now, that would solve the problem. You'd learn everything about me, and I would learn everything about you." He rose from the bed and placed his hands on my shoulders.

The warm pressure of his palms was grounding. The allure of his blue eyes jumbled the reasons we shouldn't do this now in my head. He was right. It's why Fae marked their mates as soon as they met. We all understood they destined us to be together so why prolong the inevitable of sharing everything about ourselves? Part of me wanted that, but the part holding back was the one who didn't trust him.

Why didn't I trust him?

Was it for the way he'd left me the first time we'd met? Or was there more to my fated mate that was making me hesitant?

He lowered his head and kissed me. My body melted into his. This was the connection of mates. The way they made our bodies for each other. Our minds too, so why couldn't I give him that part?

Perhaps I should give into his desire now?

His palms glowed with his powers making light shine against my closed eyelids. My powers surged to my palms again. It all felt so right. So natural as though this moment was written in time. We were meant to be here with each other.

What was I waiting for?

My hand slid toward his chest.

A knock rapped on the caravan door. Before we even stopped kissing, the door flew open, and a young woman bounded into the interior.

"Oh." She skidded to a stop.

I yanked my hands away from Fallon and stepped back as far as possible in the small interior of the caravan.

"Not now, Erin," Fallon said.

"Sorry." Erin blushed, a delicate pink stain appearing across her cheeks.

"Wait," I said. "You're Fallon's sister?"

"I am." She glanced nervously between us.

She was unearthly beautiful. A radiant glow shone from her chestnut brown hair. She had the same startling blue eyes as Fallon, but where his eyes held a wealth of knowledge hidden in the alluring depths, hers appeared more innocent.

I stepped forward. This was the woman who'd kept us apart all these years. If Fallon hadn't needed to find her, then he would have fled Earth and returned to the Summer Court with me the night we met. I wanted to hate her. I wanted to stab her with a dagger.

She exchanged a worried glance with Fallon.

"I... um... I'm sorry."

"Sorry?" I cocked an eyebrow.

"For busting in here while you two are together. I'm not used to Fallon having a mate. I promise I won't do it again."

She sounded so sweet and innocent. My curled fingers shifted away from the edge of the dagger. I twisted away from her as her words ran through my mind. It made little sense. Wouldn't Erin be acquainted with not going into her brother's caravan while he had a woman with him?

"Do you have a system in place, so you didn't interrupt him when he was with other women?"

Or did Fallon not take women back to his caravan? Why was I so hung up on my mate being with other women? The jealousy eating away at my insides hurt my stomach. I couldn't help but think about Fallon with other women.

"Fallon with other women?" Erin laughed.

"Why is that funny?" My fingers rubbed the edge of the hilt as I imagined stabbing all those other women who'd enjoyed my mate.

"Fallon hasn't been with anyone." She shot her brother a glance then continued, "Ever."

Had I heard her wrong? Or was she truly saying my mate hadn't been with a woman?

"Erin, you little turd. Why did you have to tell her that?" Fallon asked, sounding the way I did when one of my brothers or sisters annoyed me.

"What?" Erin shrugged. "She deserves to know. Plus, the look of death in her eyes when talking about other women made me want to say something."

Fallon crossed his arms and glared at his sister.

"Everyone said she stabbed you. I don't want to get stabbed too."

Fallon cocked an eyebrow.

"I'll leave you two to talk. See you at breakfast."

Erin raced out of the door.

The sudden quiet of the room made me want to say something, anything to fill it with the awkward reveal by his sister.

Fallon cleared his throat and said, "So, yeah, I'm a virgin."

# CHAPTER TEN
# FALLON

AISLINN LOOKED EMBARRASSED WHEN I should have been the one to be embarrassed at the way my sister dropped the truth of my sexual history with the grace of a baby giraffe. She opened her mouth and then closed it without saying a word. We stared at each other, me waiting for Aislinn to speak her mind, because I recognized she had something to say about my virginity.

In the end, she slid a knife from a holster and spun it around her fingers, not even breaking eye contact as she did so. As though the motion settled her mind she at last asked, "You haven't been with a woman, ever?"

"No."

"But last night you were... good."

"I've imagined doing lots of things to you."

Her eyebrows rose. "You have a vivid imagination."

"Very."

"But why haven't you had sex?" she asked.

"I couldn't have sex with another woman knowing my fated mate was alive and in the Summer Court."

"What about before we met? Wasn't there anyone then?"

"No, I was young. I'd contemplated it, but I had met no one who I'd wanted to share that with."

Her throat worked as she swallowed. She seemed at a loss for words again. Turning, she thrust the blade of the knife into the timber tabletop and sat heavily on the bench seat.

"You would have learned all this when we marked each other."

She lifted her head. "As you will learn, I'm not a virgin."

"I don't care. You're mine. And I'll have you any way possible."

"Fallon." She sighed my name.

Whatever was holding her back from our destined marking, I'd break through those walls one brick at a time.

I held out my hand, and said, "Let's eat."

Aislinn slid her hand into mine and stood, retrieving the dagger, she slid it back into the holster. Why did I find her knives sexy? Even after she'd stabbed me in the heart with them. Nothing wasn't worth the price of winning her over. Of having my fated mate by my side.

We stepped from the caravan into the brisk morning air, even though the sun streamed from the sky between the thickening clouds that would soon cover the horizon, a coolness settled through the atmosphere, not that Fae cared about the cold. Every eye around the campfire lifted to our faces. Conversation stopped as they watched us walk toward them.

Hamish stepped forward. "Morning. Good to see your wounds have healed."

The wound in my heart was still a little tender, but I said, "Yes."

There was no need to worry Hamish. Our injuries had been taking longer to heal these days, and I didn't understand why. Luckily, I was the one who had most of the injuries from my underground fighting. Everyone else had less physically demanding jobs these days so most were unaware of our healing problems. I'd just assumed it was something to do with the locked Veil, but if there was a doorway now, then wouldn't we heal at our normal rate once again?

I walked Aislinn toward a pair of chairs and motioned for her to sit. She did it with the ingrained grace of a princess. I sat beside her, and Erin walked over with two bowls in her hand. It was strange to have Aislinn sitting beside me instead of Erin. Erin's face flashed with a range of emotions before she kept walking and held the bowls out to us.

"Thank you," Aislinn said, accepting the bowl that was probably meant to be Erin's breakfast.

"You're welcome," Erin said, then turned and returned to collect another bowl for herself.

The campfire was small this morning for cooking. Porridge was our staple breakfast alongside a hot cup of brewed tea and coffee for those who'd acquired a taste for the more bitter beverage. Aislinn's gaze snagged on the flames as the flickering hypnotized her. I rubbed a hand on her thigh.

"Everything all right?"

She jumped as though her mind had been in a different time and place. Her luminous blue eyes with the indigo ring, lifted to my face. She stared at me and then blinked rapidly.

"Hey," I said, taking her bowl and setting them both on the ground. "What is it?"

"The flames," she whispered.

Understanding filled me. The night I'd met my mate flames had burned her skin. Her feet were a mess of red, blistered flesh, her dress singed, but thank Dia, her brother had rescued her before the flames had engulfed her.

I clicked my fingers. "Put out the fire."

"No," Aislinn snapped. "I'll be okay. It's... we haven't had a fire in the Summer Court since that night."

My eyebrows rose. That seemed extreme but understandable.

"You were okay last night by the campfire," I pointed out.

"Last night I was in shock, I barely noticed anything except you."

"Well, now I'm offended you're not noticing me this morning."

She let out a soft laugh.

"That's better." I smiled, cupping her face in mine, I lowered my mouth to hers unable to resist kissing her again.

The kiss was short and sweet. Nothing like I longed to do with my mate, but we had an audience. One that wouldn't stop staring at us.

"I'm serious," I said. "We can put out the fire."

"No." She shook her head and stared at the dancing orange flames. "I'll be okay. It's just, that I can't stab it."

My turn to laugh.

"What is your power?"

"Air," she said.

"So, you can blow the flames away from you. Smother them if you need to."

She lifted one shoulder. "I suppose so."

"Why don't you like using your power?"

She bent and retrieved her bowl. "I'm hungry."

I collected my bowl too. "Aislinn, help me out here, I'm trying to get to know you, but you keep blocking me."

She swallowed a spoonful of porridge. "I'm trying too."

"Okay, sweetheart." I brushed her thick braid back over her shoulder. "Slow and steady will get us there. We have eternity together now."

Her lips thinned as she shoved the next spoonful of porridge into her mouth. Past lips I wanted to kiss all day long, but I had responsibilities. She had responsibilities back in the Summer Court no doubt. Not that she'd told me any of those either. My enigmatic mate was worth waiting for though.

We ate in silence. The rest of the Fae ate making quiet conversation between themselves. No one appeared to know what to say to a Fae Princess. Aislinn didn't seem to mind their lack of interaction with her, or if she did, I didn't know her well enough to comprehend what was bothering her. I had learned a few of her tells though. The way her lips thinned. The way her fingers twitched for the hilt of the daggers strapped on her body.

I'd learn everything there was to appreciate about my mate.

Aislinn stood. "I'd like to talk to my brother."

"Of course. Do you know where he's staying?"

"I do. My guards do too."

I'd forgotten about the red-cloaked guards skulking behind us since they were so quiet it was like they didn't exist.

I stood. "Then we'll go."

"Oh no. You can stay here."

"Aislinn," I said, clasping her hand in mine. "You're my mate. Wherever you go, I go too."

Her lips firmed. I almost smiled at her tell, but she didn't deny my claim or my words so that was one more step closer to me winning her over.

"We'll be back soon," I said to everyone.

Hamish scowled, his eyes meeting mine with disapproval lingering in their depths. He needed to understand my mate came first, and that didn't mean I'd not look out for them anymore. Just that she was more important. Which to some might make me sound like an ass, but that was their problem and not mine. I was who I was, and I wouldn't apologize for my beliefs and ideas.

We walked through the forest, and I almost imagined this was a pleasant stroll with my mate, except for the guards at our back. A Fae Princess was worth protecting though. The woods cleared, and we walked to the edge of a stream. Wildflowers dotted the fields on both sides swaying in the building breeze.

"A storm is coming," I noted.

"Do you use your powers to create storms?" Aislinn asked.

"No. Not anymore."

"Why not?" She peered sideways at me.

"They're too volatile now. Are yours the same? Is that why you don't use them?"

"I couldn't say." She shrugged.

There was her ambiguous answer again. What was up with her power? As a Fae royal her powers were greater than mine, but why was she so against using hers? It made no sense. Perhaps because I loved my powers even though the force of them was becoming harder to control, I'd never stop using them. What had caused Aislinn to forsake her powers? And why would her family let her? Especially the King.

The wildflower field led into a weeping willow forest alongside the stream. The water gurgled a cheerful tune as though welcoming us along its path. Leaves from the low-hanging branches brushed against us as though testing our powers. Was there magic in this place?

The dirt path led us to a clearing with a cottage. Smoke billowed from the chimney. I'd expected to see the other Fae guards standing watch, but they weren't to be seen. The caravan and horse we'd sent over here sat a small distance away from the cottage. We walked up to the cottage door, and I knocked.

No one answered.

"Where are they?" Aislinn asked.

"Maybe they walked to our camp to find you?"

"Perhaps." Aislinn frowned.

I hated seeing her frown.

"Let's try the caravan."

One of her guards strode in front of us toward the caravan while the other followed. He walked up the wooden steps to the bright red door carved with golden horses. Not pausing to knock, he flung it open and revealed the empty interior.

"Makes sense they're not here if Prince Lorcan is absent," the guard said.

"Aye," Aislinn said. "We'll wait here for them."

"I'd prefer to wait back at my camp."

Aislinn walked toward the cottage again. It had a charming quality to it with a thatched roof and white-painted window frames. Not what I would have expected a Fae Prince and a witch to live in. Would Aislinn be amendable to living on Earth instead of in the palace in the Summer Court? We had so much to discuss, and she barely gave me any information.

She walked through the small gate, her dress blowing about her legs with the growing wind. The sky darkened ominously. Another reason I'd prefer to take her back to camp. To my caravan where we would snuggle under the warmth of the thick blanket and weather the storm in each other's arms.

Maybe I'd even lose my virginity.

I sighed and followed her into the garden, keeping a short distance from her curvaceous form. The thick braid of her hair hung down her back, too heavy for the wind to whip around her head, but if she'd left it free, it would be a curtain of living silvery blonde hair. My fingers itched to let it free. Let her experience the freedom of the breeze caressing her hair. Her tense posture told me she didn't let herself free ever. I longed to change that for my mate.

"Aislinn!"

We both turned to the sound of her brother's voice.

"About time," Aislinn muttered under her breath so only I heard.

We waited for her brother and his mate to join us in the garden.

"I hope you didn't pick anything in here," Pepper said.

Aislinn narrowed her eyes. Another one of her tells that I was growing used to seeing.

Lorcan stepped in front of his mate ever so casually that it didn't appear like he was protecting her, but it was what I would have done in his position.

"What Pepper means by that is, there are dangerous plants in her garden," Lorcan said.

"Oh." Aislinn's voice softened. "I didn't touch any plants. I was admiring the garden. We don't have one like this back home."

Pepper slid under Lorcan's arm. "The Summer Court is pretty."

"Your garden is too," Aislinn said.

Pepper's eyes flew wide as though she hadn't expected Aislinn to be nice to her.

"Where did you go?" Aislinn asked, changing the subject so fast I had whiplash.

Lorcan and Pepper exchanged worried glances.

"What is it?"

"I had a meeting with the Witches Council."

"Why?" Aislinn asked as though she'd expected something to go wrong on her trip.

"They heard Pepper had me," Lorcan said.

Pepper cackled. "Rumors run rampant amongst witches. There are still rumors about my old coven."

"What rumors?"

"A few years ago someone killed all the witches in my old coven. All except the High Priestess and a young girl not yet acquainted with her skills."

I stepped closer to Aislinn and asked, "All of them?"

Pepper nodded, her skin paling under the darkness of the growing storm.

"Who would do such a thing?" Aislinn asked.

"That's the thing," Pepper said. "The High Priestess claimed a vampire did it."

"You don't believe her?" I asked.

I didn't either. Vampires were more elusive than most supernatural creatures even though humans still liked to spread stories of their existence more than any other supernatural creature.

"No," Pepper said. "I don't trust her. Never have. She was the reason I left the coven. Good thing too otherwise I might not be here today."

"What does this have to do with us?" Aislinn asked.

Surely, she didn't say that? This was her brother's fated mate. And she wasn't concerned about someone killing her kind?

"Nothing at all to do with you," Pepper said, even though the hurt emanated in her voice.

Lorcan brushed a kiss to his mate's forehead. "Sorry. Aislinn, can I talk to you?"

She nodded and walked away with Lorcan into the cottage leaving me with Pepper and the guards at a discreet distance.

Pepper lifted the hood of her cloak from her head. "Wow, Lorcan was a hard shell to crack but Aislinn seems worse."

I laughed. "She's tough, I'll give her that."

"You'll succeed in cracking it. Fated mates are destined to cure the other's hurts."

"Cure? That's a strange word to use."

"Perhaps I should have said ease?" She rubbed her forehead and closed her eyes.

"Are you okay?"

"I'm fine." She dropped her hand. "I don't trust Miss Margo Manning, the High Priestess of my old coven."

"Seems highly unlikely a vampire would kill so many people and draw attention to themselves and the entire community."

"I agree. I'd say Miss Margo did it, but proving it is impossible. It's why the witches council is still asking questions. She's sneaky."

"She sounds it. Is the coven near here?"

"No, it's on the coast."

"Our troupe was planning on moving on soon. We'll stay away from the coast."

"Now you have an invitation to the Summer Court. Will you go?"

"I suppose I have to. Aislinn wants to return. Where she goes, so do I."

Pepper smiled. "You Fae mates are very possessive and protective."

"Is that a bad thing?"

"It's intense and can sometimes be overwhelming, but I wouldn't give Lorcan up for anything in the world."

I returned her smile. "I guess we're now part of the same family."

Pepper's smile grew even bigger. "Family is a wonderful thing to have."

I couldn't agree with her more. It was time for me to stop putting off the inevitable and go to the Summer Court even if only for the reason of meeting my mate's family.

# CHAPTER ELEVEN
## AISLINN

L ORCAN WHIRLED ON ME the second the door closed. "What is your problem?"

"Mine?"

"Aye, you." Lorcan folded his arms. "I've put up with your moods for too long. Cut you as much slack as possible considering what you went through—"

I cut him off. "Don't even say it."

His crown of thorns writhed around his head reminding me so much of father.

"We all went through so much. Don't let it drive a wedge between us now my mate is a witch."

"But..."

"No." He tapped his fingers on his arm. "She had nothing to do with the past."

I hung my head in shame. "You're right. I'm holding onto the past for no reason other than to stop feeling anything except anger." I lifted my gaze through the thickness of my lashes. "How do I let it go?"

Lorcan dropped his arms and stepped forward, giving me a quick hug he said, "Let your mate in."

"It's hard."

He rubbed my arms. "I understand. Believe me. I didn't want to mark Pepper. I didn't want her to see my memories, but she accepted me and all the darkness."

"You believe you're dark?" I asked, shocked my honorable brother would see himself that way.

"We all have our burdens to bear. Let Fallon ease yours."

What would that be like? To have someone accept me for me. For whatever shortcomings I had. To ease the hurt and pain that had been with me for too long. I stared out of the cottage window. I should let him in. Since we'd met again, he hadn't put a foot wrong to prove his loyalty to me.

Through the window, Pepper smiled as she talked with Fallon, and something clicked in my head. They were now part of our family as was Saoirse's mate Arrow, and their child Ailbhe, Briana's mate Sledge, and Rian's mate Sophia. I'd accepted them. I had to accept Pepper. And I had to accept Fallon. One day, Ciara and Roisin would have mates I'd have to accept, too.

"When did you become so smart?" I asked with a cheeky grin.

"I've always been smart." He winked.

"Should we be worried about this attack on Pepper's old coven?"

"We'll make some inquiries, but Pepper knows the most about them and she suspects the High Priestess being involved and not vampires. Either way, it has nothing to do with Fae or our powers so don't worry. Plus it was years ago."

"'Tis hard not to worry."

"All the Trappers are dead. I made sure of it." He walked into the kitchen and set a kettle on the stove.

"You seem at home here." I stepped toward him, glancing around the cozy interior of the cottage. Plants hung from various places giving an earthly atmosphere to the place. Sunlight streamed through the windows landing on the books lining the bookshelves. Throw cushions and a fluffy blanket were laid before the fireplace that held the remnants of a fire. I understood why he'd be at home here.

"It's where I waited a long time for Pepper to wake from the Quiet."

I pursed my lips. "Do you think Fallon will be in the Quiet for a long time when I mark him?"

"We can't know until you do it. Besides, you'll be in the Quiet with him since he's a Fae too and he'll mark you in the way of the Fae." The kettle whistled, and he lifted it from the stovetop. "It's strange all our fated mates have been turning out to be other supernatural creatures, but yours is a regular Fae."

I laughed. "You sound disappointed."

"I almost am." He laughed too while pouring the hot water into eight cups.

Trust my brother to think of the Fae guards too while making refreshments. He placed the cups on a tray and carried it toward the front door.

"Are you going to make yourself useful and open the door?"

I rolled my eyes. "Annoying as always."

He laughed again. I hadn't seen Lorcan this happy since he was a child. I couldn't hold on to my grudge against witches when his witch mate made him happy. What sort of sister would I be if I did? The worst and I wasn't. I didn't want to be either. I longed to experience the happiness of a fated mate too. As I opened the door for Lorcan, Fallon's gaze found mine. His lips spread into a smile as though the sight of me made him happy. If that was true, then I had all I needed for contentment right outside. So close all I had to do was let myself be open to my mate and everything he made me feel.

Lorcan passed around the cups, and everyone drank in silence. It wasn't uncomfortable either.

As soon as we finished the beverages though, Fallon asked, "When would you like to return to the Summer Court?"

I almost dropped the cup in surprise he'd ask such a question.

"As soon as possible."

He nodded. "All right, Aislinn. We'll go to the Summer Court now. Let me tell my troupe first."

"Now?" I asked, shock tinging my voice.

"Yes, now, it's what you want." He lifted the cup from my hands and placed them on the tray on the ground. "My mate gets whatever she wants."

My lips spread into a smile of their own making. "That might turn out bad for you."

"Never." He smiled.

A warm fluttering sensation burst to life in my chest. Fallon clasped his palm to mine in a hold that said you're mine, and I'll cherish you.

Turning to Lorcan, I said, "Will you return to the Summer Court?"

"In a day or two," Lorcan said.

"I'll see you then." I turned to Pepper, and said, "Keep an eye on Lorcan. He's always getting up to mischief and he'll need you to keep him in line since I won't be here."

Pepper cackled like a witch and the sound didn't send me into instant hate.

"Tell me about it," she said. "We'll see you soon, then you can take over so I can have a break."

I laughed. Perhaps I'd judged the witch too harshly. She had a sassy streak to her that I identified with.

We walked back the way we'd come. The air cooled even more when the thick clouds cut off all signs of the sun. The wind was so harsh now that we struggled to walk into the headwind. As we emerged through the forest close to the camp, the first heavy drops of rain fell onto our heads. Fallon tugged me into a run, and we raced through the pounding rain and into the warmth of his caravan.

Fallon slammed the door closed and leaned against it, his muscular chest heaving after our thrilling run. Mine lifted with every sharp inhale. His gaze dropped to my chest, heating with desire in an instant. I glanced down at the damp fabric which was now see-through. My nipples were dark against the translucent fabric. Hard and growing harder every second Fallon stared at them. Desire curled lower in my stomach.

My mate was a virgin. The knowledge made me want him even more. Made me want to share his first time with him. I couldn't believe he'd waited centuries for me to experience sex. My gaze dipped from his chest to the firm planes of his stomach plastered with his wet t-shirt. His many fights to blow off steam, while a good alternative outlet for his energy, had added to the many muscles on his body. His brutality added to his appeal in a heady masculine display of strength. Lower still I let my gaze wander, to the growing length of him behind his pants.

I licked the rain from my lips as water dripped from my braid down my face. Stepping forward, I slid my palms against his tight stomach. He sucked in a ragged breath. My fingers found the buttons on his pants and popped them free.

"What are you doing?" he asked on a ragged breath.

"Waiting out the storm." I curled my hand around his cock.

He dropped his head back against the wooden door. "It'll last awhile yet."

"Plenty of time then."

"For what?" His hands curled into fists at his side as though he wanted to touch me, but I hadn't permitted him yet.

"For your first."

He groaned. "But I want to mark you first."

"Again, with the marking." I squeezed his cock earning a drop of liquid in the warmth of my palm. "Why that first? Why can't we share our bodies first?"

"Anything you want." He closed his eyes.

I paused my caress on his cock. "Why?" I whispered.

His eyes opened, and the expression in his glassy blue depths about dropped me to my knees.

"I want your heart as well as your body."

"Oh."

"I want our first time to mean more than a frenzied passion of fated mates coming together," he rasped out, his hips moving as though he couldn't take my hand on his cock any longer.

"But me touching you is all right."

"Never stop touching me."

I tugged his pants down around his hips with my other hand not giving up my grasp on his firm cock for anything. When his pants revealed the true size of his cock, my insides turned to liquid heat. I longed to impale myself on his hard length. To have him buried deep inside me. I shivered from the image dancing behind my eyes. I stroked his cock, getting a sense of the smooth flesh covering the steel underneath. His eyes slammed shut as he let out a ragged groan.

"Do you like that?" I asked.

He choked on a laugh. "What do you think?"

"Hmm, I think we can make this first time better." I slid to my knees.

"Dia, Aislinn." He groaned my name like I was a goddess.

"Aye?" I peered up at his quivering body.

His heated gaze hit me full force in the face. So much want lay in his hungry eyes. My mouth watered to give him this. The same way he'd given to me last night. How had that been his first time giving oral pleasure? I wanted to make this good for him. I swept a soft kiss to the head of his cock. His knees shook. I swiped my tongue along the length of his cock leaving a trail of moisture behind. He let out another ragged groan.

My lips parted, and I swallowed him into the depths of my mouth. Placing my hand on his buttocks, I urged him to thrust his cock into my mouth. To use me for his pleasure. I wanted to make him come undone. To see him shake and cry out my name with his release. I kept my gaze on his rapt face. Each motion thrust him deeper into my throat. I softened my jaw. His gaze never left my face as though he couldn't believe I was kneeling before him and giving him pleasure.

My core wept with the need to have him inside me. I tightened my hold on him, digging my fingernails into the hard globes of his butt cheeks. It was pleasant torture having him but not where I wanted him most. I let out a moan thinking about the way he'd thrust into me. His cock jerked in my mouth. He'd liked my moan. His hands slid down to the side of my face and cupped my cheeks.

"Dia, you're so beautiful."

I almost wept with the emotion in his voice. This was so different from any other time I'd performed oral sex on a man. Before it'd been about sexual gratification. Now, it was about a connection.

About feelings for my mate.

Feelings he had for me.

He slowed his thrusts, savoring each moment of our connection, but it made me more needy. I wriggled closer to Fallon, so the tips of my nipples brushed against his legs as he slowly thrust into my mouth. His hands warmed on my cheeks. The clasp was firm but gentle. A claiming hold letting me comprehend I wasn't going anywhere. Not that I would. Or that I wanted to. That realization made my heart thud inside my chest. I wanted and needed Fallon to take care of me. Tears welled in my eyes. How did he take this moment of heated pleasure and turn it into emotion?

My emotions spilled more into my chest until my entire heart glowed with a new kind of heat. This man of mine would be my greatest love. My greatest treasure. As I would be his.

His thighs tensed. Under my hand, his balls tightened even harder. One thrust later, he came with a groan so deep, I sensed it in my womb. Dia, I wanted to hear him groan like that while filling me. He released into the back of my throat, his eyes slamming shut against the pleasure wracking his body in great quivers of ecstasy. I gulped down everything he gave to me because he was mine.

And I'd have all of him.

I'd put that look of thrall on his face. His eyes snapped open, and he slid his cock from my mouth, wiping the small mess that followed from my lips. He slid his hands under my arms and hoisted me to my feet then hugged me to his chest.

"Thank you," he whispered into my ear.

I chuckled. "Thank you?"

"Yes. That was... no words can describe the way you just made me feel."

I snuggled into his hold. This was good. So good. I felt good about myself. About my growing feelings for Fallon. Confident we would make a future for ourselves as mates. I slid my arms around his neck and held on. I'd never let him go. Now I understood what he was saying with his words. I had the same sentiments now too.

A knock clanged on the door behind his head. Fallon gave me a wry smile as I shifted out of his embrace. He shoved himself back in his pants and wrapped a blanket around my shoulders before opening the door.

"Hamish? What is it?" Fallon asked.

"Sorry to interrupt." Hamish glared between Fallon and me. No doubt seeing our rumpled state. "It's Erin."

"What about her?" he asked.

Hamish grimaced. "She's missing."

# CHAPTER TWELVE

## AISLINN

FEAR SHOT THROUGH MY system like a bolt of liquid ice. Fallon's sister was missing. Was it my fault? I shoved the notion down. How was it my fault? I barely knew the woman. Barely understood my mate if I was honest.

"Don't stress, she'll be back," Fallon said.

"What?" I gasped.

"She does a runner every time we've decided it's time to move on." He rubbed his chin. "She'll be back."

"But there's a storm out." I pointed to the raging weather beyond the cozy comfort of the caravan.

"Yes, and knowing Erin, she's likely shacked up with that Rory fella she's been hanging around the last few months."

Hamish scowled, not in my direction for once but at Fallon's words.

"Don't fret." He rubbed my shoulders over the blanket. "We'll go to the Summer Court as soon as the storm breaks. Nothing will change between us, I promise."

The sudden surg of guilt made my throat thicken, and I couldn't swallow. Could I ask Fallon to leave Earth when his sister was missing? I don't think I had it in me to demand he leave with me now. He should stay and find her.

"No." He shook his head. "I'm not leaving your side."

How had he read my mind?

"Hamish? Is what Fallon saying true that Erin will turn up? Or should we be worried about her safety?"

Hamish's scowl darkened. "It's true. The little shite always forms connections with humans and then when it's time for us to leave she throws a hissy fit."

"See." Fallon rubbed my shoulders again. "Nothing to worry about."

Hamish opened the door and slammed it behind him. I frowned at his retreating form. He didn't appear happy that Erin was missing. But then again, she wasn't a child and if she was off with a man, then who were we to tell her who she could and couldn't be with?

"She lets humans court her?"

Fallon chuckled. "Such an old-fashioned way of saying it."

I tilted my head to the side. "How would you say it then?"

"She ah... dates them." His cheeks flushed red.

His embarrassment was endearing.

"She has sex with humans?"

His face reddened even more. "Yes."

"Well." I folded my arms over my chest. What did I say to that?

Silence stretched between us until I said, "My sister Saoirse used to have sex with humans while in heat so she avoided falling pregnant."

Fallon's eyebrows rose over the surprise in his eyes. "How did that go for her?"

I shrugged. "I suppose it was pragmatic until it wasn't."

"How so?"

"She ended up pregnant to a wolf shifter."

Fallon attempted to say something, but he spluttered his words together. Dia, he was even more adorable than I first considered with his blush. He slid his fingers into my hair and cupped the back of my head.

"I can't wait to see your memories. They sound like they'll be interesting."

"And yours?" I asked. "Are yours interesting?"

"I like to think they are." He stepped closer and drew me toward his firm chest.

My body melted into his as though we were magnets drawn together and couldn't stand to be apart.

"Thank you for what you did earlier."

I lifted my chin. He lowered his head and brushed a soft kiss on my lips.

"I never realized it would be so... there isn't a word to describe the way you made me feel."

He stared into my eyes as though I was a goddess and, in that moment, I sensed the unconditional devotion of my mate. The way he'd put me first before his sister this time echoed in my head making more of the walls around my heart crumble. He lowered his head and kissed me again. The sweetness behind the way his lips stirred against mine was even better than the way he gazed at me.

I jerked back as a sudden thought hit me. "But what about the coven attack?"

"What about it?"

"Aren't you worried Erin might be in trouble?"

He scoffed. "No. If vampires drained the witches, it was because they deserved it. You understand as well as I do the way witches work."

"I do, but my brother has mated with a witch now. I'm concerned."

He brushed a hand over my cheek. "Vampires don't slaughter a group of people for no reason and leave evidence of their existence."

"So, you're saying a vampire didn't do it?"

He rolled his massive shoulders. "If a vampire did it, then it was at the master vampire's orders and if it was a vampire on a rogue killing spree, then the vampire bounty hunters will take care of them. We have nothing to worry about."

"I wish I had your carefree attitude," I said wriggling out of his hold and lifting the curtain at the window.

"I've lived here a long time, Aislinn." Certainty filled his voice. "I comprehend what a threat to us is and what isn't." His warm body shifted closer to my back.

"The storm is blowing over. The wind has dropped, and the rain isn't as heavy."

My fingers clutched the thick fabric of the curtain in a tight grip. My stomach churned and my nerves spiked through my body about being here. We shouldn't leave here when his sister was missing.

I blew a long breath out of my lips. The warmth of my breath hit the cool glass of the window and formed a thick white fog.

"Relax." He stretched over me and drew the curtain closed. "Erin is fine. Shacked up in a warm bed no doubt."

I spun around. "I still can't believe you're a virgin."

He chuckled. "Well, hopefully not for long."

My lips twitched at his hopeful tone and the way his gaze never strayed from me as though he wanted to study every flicker of emotion in my face.

"But then again, we can do more of that earlier stuff while we're waiting. I won't complain about that," he said with a cheeky grin.

I laughed. My heart was well and truly getting lightened with every moment I spent with my mate. Perhaps when we were in the safety of the Summer Court, I'd let the last walls down and we would mark each other. Learn all there was to know about our pasts.

The barrage of the rain on the roof stopped as though someone had flipped a switch. The storm had passed as abruptly as it had started. A bit like our growing affection for each other had started quickly, but being fated mates meant it would never pass. This was it for us forever.

Forever was a long time.

But would it be forever when our Spring of Life might end soon and with it our immortality? What would Fallon say when he learned that truth?

He threaded his fingers through mine. "Stop worrying." He lifted them to his lips and kissed the knuckles. "Erin will be fine."

So he kept saying. Was he saying it for himself? Was he worried and hiding it from me? If I knew my mate better, then I'd understand, but as I didn't, I'd only guess what he was thinking and feeling. But he'd picked up on the minor change in me to realize I was worried about something. He might have said the wrong thing but at least he was paying attention to me. To what made me tick.

"We should go." I tugged his hand toward the door.

Dropping the blanket from my shoulders, we stepped out of the door and into the moisture-laden air. The fresh rain smell on the soil was thick and refreshing. I drew in a deep inhale. Earth had its positives, and its weather was one of them. My guards jumped to attention from under the porch of the nearest caravan. They strode toward us, their red cloaks blowing behind them with the breeze still whipping through the place. The rain might have stopped, but the weather was still harsh.

I drew on my royal powers influencing the Veil. Doors flew open to every caravan as the Fae stepped onto their porches and stared with avid interest at seeing the Veil after many years of not having access to it.

"I forgot," Fallon said, awe tinging his voice.

"Forgot what?"

"The beauty and power."

The purple curtain parted for us. I stepped into the Veil, and my guards followed. Fallon stared at us, his lips parted, his eyes wide. He seemed frozen in place. Was all the talk about coming with me a lie?

My hands touched the hilt of my daggers. Perhaps I'd stab him in the heart again, because if he'd broken down my walls only to hurt me again...

# CHAPTER THIRTEEN
# FALLON

To watch Aislinn use her powers to open the Veil was a staggering sight to see. She was beautiful before but now standing in the misty magic she was exquisite. A beauty no one or nothing could rival. I couldn't move. Didn't want to. I wanted to stare at my mate for as long as possible without blinking.

But then her eyes hardened.

What was I doing gaping in awe at my mate when I should have been by her side?

I strode toward her, eager to venture to the Summer Court. To be by her side wherever she'd take me. My fingers curled around hers. Her magic tickled against my palm as I held her hand in mine. What would it feel like when she used her powers to mark me?

"You are so beautiful, never more so than when using your powers," I whispered in her ear.

Her head jerked to the side as if I'd shocked her with my words. Her gaze darted to my eyes as if she read the validity of my statement in them. It was true. Every word.

"See, you do use your powers." My lips brushed the shell of her ear as I leaned closer and whispered the words.

She shivered. Finally, a sign I was getting to my mate.

"Will you mark me in the Summer Court?" I asked, way too eagerly.

The guard's heads snapped toward us.

Aislinn narrowed her eyes. "We'll see."

Always so hesitant. For once, I longed for Aislinn to jump toward me headfirst and not let her fear hold her back that I wouldn't catch her.

The Veil parted, and the guards stepped out. I planted a quick kiss on Aislinn's lips, her surprise parting them and making me wish to deepen the kiss instead of meeting the King. I shoved the urge back and let Aislinn walk out of the Veil.

Then drawing in a centering breath, I followed Aislinn through the open doorway of the tower into the direct radiant beams of sunlight. Sunshine beamed on my face. Golden and light. Joyful. That was the way it made me feel. The beams caressed my skin as though learning who I was. A soft breeze ruffled the edges of my hair. Many of the King's guards stood around the building.

They had swords strapped to them, as though they were ready to fight a foe walking through the Veil.

I wasn't an enemy. And I'd never fight another Fae. Since all we had was our troupe and we'd formed a family of sorts, I'd never hurt them.

As for humans, I didn't have a problem beating them to pulp for money.

"Who is this?" A Fae stepped forward with a scroll in one hand and a quill in the other.

"Fallon O'Sullivan," I said.

His steely blue eyes assessed me from head to toe.

"We found him and a few other Fae in England, but he was the only one who would come," Brogan, Aislinn's guard, said.

The scribe's lips became a non-existent line.

"The others will come in time," I said.

"I see." He wrote on the scroll and then tucked it under his arm. "The King is awaiting your arrival."

"Already?" Aislinn asked.

"He's been waiting for your return since you left, Your Highness."

I threaded my fingers through Aislinn's, earning another disgruntled look from the scribe. Aislinn dismissed the guards who attempted to convince her to let them accompany us to the palace, but she was steadfast in her stubbornness. It was good to see it wasn't just directed at me. Aislinn spun on her heel and marched away from the tower. I took one last look at the tall structure in the middle of nowhere with its red roof before striding after her and catching up to Aislinn with my long legs.

"Do you remember the Summer Court?" she asked.

"I've never been here."

She stopped so suddenly that her dress flapped about her legs. I paused and turned back to face her.

"What?" she whispered.

"I never traveled here."

"'Tis strange," she said then started walking again.

"Not really," I shrugged, falling into step with her once again. "My family, our entire village were happy on Earth. I think a few traveled here sometimes."

Her silence spoke about the way she was thinking. I'd learned that about her too in our short time together. I stared at all the unfamiliar sights before me. Crops so tall they stretched above my head, golden stalks rustled in the breeze. Beyond the crops lining the dirt path were trees larger than I'd seen. Their leaves shone gold in the sunshine. Butterflies in a variety of colors fluttered across the path as the crops gave way to a section of wildflowers. The perfumed air was heavy with Fae magic. Everywhere I looked, every piece of this place vibrated with a magical power that made my power hum in my hands. For the first time in a very long time, my power didn't feel volatile. Safe inside the Summer Court, calmness soothed the depths of me. That was the word for here. As beautiful as the Summer Court was, it was the calm and peace of the realm that soothed everything inside me. I let out a long, drawn-out sigh.

"What's wrong?" Aislinn asked.

"Nothing." I threw my hands wide. "There is nothing wrong here, and it's wonderful."

Her mouth opened and then snapped shut.

"I guess even after the King killed all the Trappers, we never felt safe on Earth. Here you don't need to worry about that, do you?"

"No," she said.

"It's hard being on Earth and having to hide my powers all the time." I lifted my hands and let my powers flow a little until they glowed. "Here I can be me."

Aislinn sighed, but before I asked why she was sighing, the palace appeared. As though from a fairytale the structure rose in a glistening display of carefully built perfection.

"Even your palace is magical."

"That would be the spring inside."

"The Spring of Life?"

"Aye," she said. "The Fae royals are the spring's protectors. It's our sacred duty."

"Does that mean you have to stay here? In the palace?"

She frowned. "I'm no longer sure. My brothers and two sisters are on Earth with their fated mates now."

"So, there's a chance we can travel between the realms?"

She squared her shoulders as the front door opened. A man stepped forward.

"Grier." Aislinn nodded. "This is Fallon O'Sullivan."

I held my hand out to the man, but he stared at my outstretched palm with disdain.

"The King is in his study."

Aislinn's fingers stroked the hilt of one of her daggers. Did she not like this man? Why else was she reaching for the daggers?

"Thank you, Grier," Aislinn said in a buttery sweet voice as her fingers fell back to her side.

Perhaps it wasn't this Fae she didn't like.

"Follow me," she said to me.

She strode along the marble hallway so fast, I didn't take in any of the décor. Aislinn paused outside a closed wooden door, drew in a long breath, and raised her hand to knock. A mumbled sound came from inside. She swung the door inward.

The Fae King sat behind a desk, his head bowed in a defeated manner. The expression as he raised his head to our presence was one I'd seen often in the mirror staring back at me.

Regret sat heavily on the King's face.

# CHAPTER FOURTEEN
## AISLINN

"FATHER, ARE YOU ALL right?" I asked. A bundle of nerves swirled inside my stomach.

"I can't fix it anymore with my powers," he said, the despair in his voice echoed inside the study.

Rushing forward, I placed my hand on his drooped shoulder. "What do you mean?"

He shook his head as if any movement was too difficult for him to manage.

"The spring." His eyes beseeched mine. "It's almost..." He gulped.

"No," I said.

I couldn't believe it. The spring couldn't stop. We'd die like human mortals if it did. And now I'd found my mate...

"No. I'll fix it. We all will fix it before..." I peered at Fallon standing in the doorway.

He'd become a silent statue the moment I'd opened the door, and I'd almost told him what was wrong with the Spring of Life. What would he say when he learned of the Fae problems? I refocused on my father. The despair rolling off him was an emotion I was well acquainted with, but he'd given us hope for a better future.

"There is hope." I squeezed his shoulder with my hand. "Don't give up."

Father stretched up and cupped my cheek. "I'd never give up on any of you. You children and your mother are my sole reason for everything."

"I'm beginning to understand." I covered his hand with mine. "When was the last time you slept?"

The dark rings under his eyes and the drawn expression on his face led me to believe it was a long time.

He frowned. "I don't remember."

"Come now," I said sliding my hand under his arm and urging him to his feet. "'Tis past the time for you to sleep."

"But there's so much to do and so little time left. I always believed we'd have forever."

"We will." I kept tugging him, urging him toward the door that was now empty of Fallon.

Where had he disappeared to?

"Grier!" I yelled into the hollow hallway.

Father's aide rushed forward seemingly from nowhere. The man had a knack for that.

"Oh dear," Grier said, sliding his arm around the other side of Father.

"Take him to his bed chambers," I said. "I'll fetch Mother."

Grier nodded and muttered to Father as they walked along the long marble hallway. Fallon reappeared as though he too had come from thin air, but the relief pouring through my body at the sight of him made my hands shake.

"Where did you go?" I snapped.

"Right here." He pointed at a large painting, one Roisin had painted of the forest.

I eyed the picture curiously then refocused on the urgent concerns of Father.

"The King wasn't how I expected him to be," Fallon said.

"I've never seen him like that," I admitted. "I need to find Mother. She'll help him fall asleep."

"How so?" he asked, falling into step with me.

"Mother has an unusual power in her voice. She can sing him to sleep."

Fallon's eyebrows rose. "Fae don't have powers like that."

My steps faltered, but then I kept walking. Mother was Fae. Her parents were Fae. She appeared Fae. What else might she be?

"Well, she does," I snapped.

Fallon side-eyed me but kept from asking more questions. Thankfully, he didn't ask about the spring.

"How do we find her in a place this big?" he asked after a lengthy pause.

"At this time of day, she'll be in the rose garden watching Roisin paint."

Fallon stared at all the hallways and doorways as though he longed to follow every single one and see what was behind every door. I attempted to see the palace from the perspective of someone new, but I failed. The palace was home.

As we approached the glass doors leading to the terrace, loud voices echoed from beyond. What was happening? I rushed outside and found Roisin flinging paint at the canvas while yelling. Mother stood back with her hands on her hips.

"Take that," Roisin said loudly flinging more paint at the canvas.

I rushed forward and grabbed Roisin's arms before she flung more paint over the perfect picture of a rose in bloom.

"What are you doing?"

"I'm letting my creativeness flow. What do you think?"

The painting had red globes of paint splattered across the flower underneath. It looked like a bloody rose, as though someone had murdered it. I suppressed a shiver at the eerie image.

"It's..." I didn't know what to say, so I settled on saying, "Different."

"I like it," she said with a massive grin on her face. "I've been helping Ciara in the library and discovered an entire section on human artists. Fascinating. I want to explore other techniques."

"Why were you yelling though?"

"Because it felt appropriate." She shrugged and turned her attention to Fallon. "Who are you?"

Straight to the point. Mother stepped forward, wiping drops of paint from her face as she did so and leaving red smears across her cheeks.

"Fallon O'Sullivan," he said.

"We found the Earth-living Fae," I said.

"Where are the rest?" Mother asked.

"They wouldn't come," I said.

Mother's pretty blonde brows puckered.

"They will in time," Fallon said. "It was a bit much for us to learn of the new doorway after being locked out for so long."

"I can't imagine," Mother said. "I'm sorry you had to endure that."

"Mother," I cut in before she interrogated my newfound mate whom I had yet to claim. "Father needs you to sing to him. Did you realize he hasn't been sleeping?"

She sighed. "I've tried, but even my powers won't fix what ails him."

My mother always fixed things. How could she not fix Father?

"I'm sorry, Fallon, we will have to talk later as I must see to my mate."

"I understand," Fallon said. "A mate is important."

"Aye," Mother said and left the rose garden at a brisk walk.

"So," Roisin said. "What's the story?"

"Story?" Fallon asked.

"Between you two." She pointed her paint-smeared finger at us.

"No story," I said at once.

"Come now," Fallon said. "Your fated mate isn't a story? And why aren't you introducing me as your fated mate?"

Warmth flooded my cheeks.

Roisin grinned. "Aislinn found her fated mate! Do Mother and Father realize? Of course not. I was right here when you met her." She giggled. "I can't wait for you to tell them. They'll be so happy for you."

My blush heated to the temperature of an inferno. Could flesh fall off from a blush?

"I'm not sure if I'll claim him yet."

Roisin gasped. "Why ever not?"

"I have my reasons." I folded my arms over my chest.

"No, Aislinn, no. I may be the youngest, but I understand what's right and wrong. Not claiming your fated mate is wrong. So very wrong. Why do you think they're fated for us in the first place?"

I hadn't given the why much thought to be honest. We all craved to find the one destined for us, but why were we fated to be together?

"I imagine the Gods playing chess with us. Moving us around until they find a perfect solution," Fallon said.

"Exactly." Roisin nodded. "Your mate is smart. Claim him now."

"But Father is not well."

"Was he that bad?"

"I've never seen him so distraught apart from that night he almost lost Mother." I shut off those memories because I didn't want to go there. "Besides, even if I wanted to, we can't mark each other right now."

"What other excuses do you want to come up with?" Fallon asked.

"Your sister for one. I still can't believe we left when she was missing."

"I told you before, she's not missing. She'll be with the young human man she's grown close to."

"We should have checked first." I rubbed my temple. "I feel bad for making you come here when you're not sure if your sister is safe."

"Trust me, she'll be safe with Rory. The man loves her."

"Awe, young love," Roisin said. "Mother's family had Fae who fell in love with humans. I don't see the issue here Aislinn. Love is love, no matter who it's with."

I scowled. "That is not my problem. It's not knowing where she is."

"We didn't know where you were while you were on Earth. How is that different?"

Fallon choked with a laugh. "She has you there."

I aimed my scowl at him.

"Stop being so damn smart for such a young age."

"You can throw up as many roadblocks as you like, Aislinn, but one day we *will* mark each other. I give you my word on that."

# CHAPTER FIFTEEN

# FALLON

“**I**F IT WILL MAKE you feel better, we can return to
Earth and find Erin,” I said.

Aislinn’s expression softened as the tight skin around
her eyes and mouth eased.

“Aye, it would make me feel better.” She dropped
the hand rubbing her temple to her side. Her fingers
automatically going to the hilt of the closest dagger.
“Should I leave when Father is not himself though?”

“More excuses,” Roisin said.

I liked her younger sister. She was quirky but had a
strong back bone. As stubborn as her sister too.

“We’ll be back before he’s woken from his nap.”

Or whatever the Fae King was going to do right now. He didn't look like the iron-fisted ruler I'd built him up to be in my mind. I'd never met him when he was the only prince as that was before my birth, and I'd been too young to care about royalty and politics as I'd preferred to run wild through the village and the nearby forest. My father took me on his boat in the small harbor. Life had been simple but enjoyable. I'd never dreamed of magical realms. Palaces. Or a princess so beautiful she made my heart thud.

"Fine," Aislinn ground out. "Brogan and Conlan will have to come back with us though."

"I'm not opposed to you having guards."

"And yet you say your sister is safe."

"My sister doesn't have a crown of flowers on her head."

"He has a point," Roisin said.

"Shh." Aislinn waved a finger at her sister.

Roisin laughed.

"I won't teach you how to throw daggers anymore," Aislinn said.

Roisin shrugged. "Saoirse is teaching me how to fight with a sword like her."

My lips twitched. Who were these blood thirsty princesses?

"I can paint better than that." Aislinn pointed at the painting.

Roisin's bottom lip wobbled.

"Aislinn," I ground out her name through clenched teeth. How could she be mean to her sister when she was trying to help?

Roisin lifted her waterlogged eyes to my face.

"Don't make your sister cry," I said.

"She will not cry." Aislinn huffed. "Trust me, I recognize her tactics. It's why she's Father's favorite because she knows how to twist him around her little finger."

"That's not true," Roisin said, the tears vanishing from her eyes in an instant.

Was she that good of an actress? Had she fooled me?

"I'm the favorite because I'm the youngest. Father still thinks of me as his baby even though I'm fifty years old." She started packing up her paintbrushes and paints.

I glanced between the two sisters. We couldn't leave when they were like this. I placed a hand on the hollow of Aislinn's back and urged her forward. She shot me a look that either meant she was about to have a go at me or her sister.

Roisin spun. "He met Mother when she was fifty."

Aislinn's lips twitched. "I know."

"So he knows damn well I'm no baby."

"Of course not. We all do."

"You don't. You all treat me like a child still." She snapped the painting case shut and lifted it from the stand. "For once it would be nice to be treated like my opinions matter."

"Roisin, they do matter. They matter to me," Aislinn said, emotion filling her voice.

Roisin paused. Stared into Aislinn's face, then nodded.

"Mark your mate then."

Whatever passed over Aislinn's face made Roisin scowl. She walked away without another word leaving the large canvas on the stand in the middle of the rose garden. I placed a hand on Aislinn's elbow. She didn't budge. Didn't flinch at the contact either. I stepped closer to my mate and wrapped my arms around her from behind. She dropped her head back onto my chest and let me offer her comfort.

And I believed my family had problems.

I suppose being a Fae royal had more difficulties than a regular family. There appeared to be a lot going on in the Summer Court that I didn't know of. I wouldn't be familiar with them until Aislinn trusted me enough to tell me or when she marked me.

Whichever would come first was the question.

I had a hunch both depended on each other. What more did I need to do to earn her trust?

"I'm sorry you haven't had a warm welcome to the Fae kingdom," Aislinn said. "I understand how much your opinion of this place matters to the others in your troupe."

"My opinion of the King and the Summer Court will only hold so much weight to the others. They have minds of their own and will form their own opinions. They need to come here for themselves."

She turned in my embrace and wrapped her arms around my waist, lowering her head to my chest, she laid it there over the constant pounding in my chest whenever I was with her. I wanted her to place her mark on me. Distracting myself, I glanced up at a flock of birds passing across the blue sky. Their rainbow-colored feathers made them seem even more special.

"What type of birds are those?" I asked. "I've never seen them before."

Aislinn lifted her head. "They're Feinics."

"Sounds close to Phoenix."

Aislinn laughed. "Because that's what they are."

My eyebrows rose. "Mythical birds?"

"Not mythical. You see them living here. The Spring Court has them too," Aislin said.

"Don't they die and rise from their ashes?"

"They don't die. That part is a myth. They're immortal like us." She glanced away. "They're impervious to fire. Perhaps that's where that myth originated from."

I brushed her hair away from her neck. "What other surprises do you have here?"

Goose bumps broke out over her exposed skin and a shiver ran down her back.

"Probably too many to tell you about."

"Secrets too?" I lifted one eyebrow.

"Aye, I have plenty of those."

I traced my finger over the soft contours of her collarbone. "One day you'll share them."

"Perhaps," she whispered.

I leaned down and placed a delicate kiss on her bared shoulder. "I guarantee it."

My lips traveled up her neck sending tiny shivers of delight in their wake. At least my mate trusted me enough with her body. I grazed the contours of her jaw with my lips, and she tilted her head giving me better access to the soft skin underneath. I kissed and nuzzled until her nipples hardened against my chest. Until her breath fell in shallow pants. Only then did I kiss her mouth. She opened to me in an instant. Welcomed me into the warm haven of her kiss. We kissed for what seemed hours and I didn't mind in the least that this here was all she was willing to give me.

I'd take whatever from her at any moment of any day, for each step brought us closer together. Closer to the moment we'd mark each other and seal our fate together forever.

The moment couldn't come soon enough for me, but at least we had eternity together to figure out a way for me to gain her trust before she marked me. I stopped kissing her little by little, coming back for another kiss each time I considered it would be the last.

She tugged my hand and drew me through the rows upon rows of roses. The heady perfumed scent of the blooms filled my lungs with each inhale. Aislinn walked so fast, I had a hard time keeping up with her.

"What's the rush?" I asked.

She threw me a seductive smirk.

I wet my lips. My blood zinged with electricity. Every nerve ending came alive when I was with her. It was as though my power responded to her. The faster we walked, the closer the structure in the distance became.

Steps led up to a gazebo as though made from the roses climbing up the pillars. Pink blooms lined the open roof and made the sunlight spilling inside a delicate pastel pink color. The way it hit Aislinn's cheeks suited her. She was even more ethereal when she blushed, but this wasn't a blush, this was the magic of the Summer Court.

As we stepped through the opening, the timber limbs of the roses closed behind us sealing us inside the gazebo. Anticipation hung heavy in the air.

"This place." I shook my head. "You."

Aislinn half smiled. "I've never seen the roses move by themselves. It's as though they know we want privacy."

"Privacy?" I cocked an eyebrow. "Whatever for?"

She laughed. That was so much better than the way she'd sounded so upset with her sister.

"Do that again," I said, stepping closer and drawing her into my arms.

"What?" she frowned.

"Laugh. Your laughter is more magical than the Summer Court."

She laughed. Her eyes lit with a luminous quality. The soft pink bathing her, made me want to strip her naked.

"Can I see you?"

"I'm right here."

"Naked?" I asked. "I've dreamed of you for so long."

Her pink tongue darted out to her lips. She drew the shoulders of her dress lower until the bare skin of her chest met my hungry eyes. The delicate expanse of her skin made my fingers itch with the need to touch her. To find out if her skin was as soft as her hair. Her hands tugged the dress lower. Her bare breasts came into view. Dusky pink nipples pebbled into tight buds under my gaze. I let out a moan.

"More?" she asked.

"All of it." I nodded.

She eased the dress down her waist, over the curve of her hips then dropped it into a pool of silken fabric at her feet. My throat went dry. She was even more beautiful and desirable than I imagined. My gaze raked her from head to foot multiple times.

"Do I live up to your dream?" she asked, a tinge of uncertainty in her voice.

"You surpassed it." I grinned and met her searching gaze. "Never did I imagine you'd have blades strapped to your body."

She laughed again. Seeing the deadly daggers strapped against her pale skin did unexpected things to my already rock-hard cock. I'd felt the sharpness of her blades. Experienced the sting behind them, but for some unknown reason seeing them on her turned me on.

"Touch me," she whispered.

She didn't need to tell me twice. I strode forward and cupped her face in my hands. Lowering my mouth to hers, I kissed her with all the desire I'd had for her since the day we'd met. She met me stroke for stroke. Kissed me as though she too had the same desire. Our bodies spoke a language of their own and that was the language of fated mates.

I lowered my hands, running my fingertips over her collarbone. Goose bumps pebbled over her skin. Lower

I let my fingers glide until they were stroking the soft mounds of her breasts. Her goose bumps doubled in size. I cupped her breasts in my hands, holding the weight in my palms while my thumbs strummed her tight nipples. She moaned and inched closer. A second later, her warm palm slid inside my pants and surrounded my hard cock.

Wetness seeped from the tip into her palm. She used it to pump my length until my legs shook and threatened to collapse from under me.

Her touch on my aroused flesh obliterated everything from my mind apart from her. She kissed me again. Her tongue twirling with mine. I dropped the hold I had on her breasts, as I needed her closer to me. Every curvaceous limb. I cupped her bottom and dragged her against my heaving chest. Her hips rolled in time with the thrusting of her hand. She lifted her legs and wrapped them around my waist. I supported her weight in the strength of my hands. Her slick center lined up with my throbbing cock. My cock thrust against her hand eager for the slick wetness between her legs. But I meant what I said, I wanted her heart before we shared our bodies. It was the only way I'd know for sure she trusted me.

"Aislinn." I groaned rolling my hips in time to hers.

She rocked against me, throwing her head back. I dipped my head to her throat and suckled the skin on her neck into my mouth. She moaned and writhed against me, her muscles tightening in my embrace. I was too far gone to make sure this was good for her too, but the way she was panting and grinding her hips led me to believe she was enjoying this too.

As if to prove she was, Aislinn's limbs shook as she cried out my name in a husky voice. She quivered against my hard cock sending me over the edge too. I released into the warmth of her palm spilling my cum over her hand too.

We stopped moving letting the waves of our release settle into a peaceful calm once again. Aislinn stepped back rubbing my release into her palms while smiling her seductive smile at me. She was so sexy and beautiful. I tucked my semi-hard cock back into my pants and watched her slide her dress back on her body covering up the stunning beauty of my mate.

I almost wanted her to run around naked, but it wouldn't be practical. I'd most likely pummel the face of any man who saw her this way.

There was so much I wanted to say to her, instead, I said, "Let's find my sister."

# CHAPTER SIXTEEN
# AISLINN

I'D NEVER ARGUED WITH Roisin before today. The fact she was unsettled and so out of sorts said more about the spring than Father's admission. Tensions were high between me and Roisin and seeing them from the perspective of my newfound mate status made them even clearer. It also made me understand the tensions in his troupe on Earth.

We couldn't go on like this.

While the release of sexual tension in the gazebo with Fallon had helped, it was the way he looked at me and spoke to me that helped settle my churning emotions. I should trust him enough to tell him everything. To mark him. But if I was in the Quiet, how would I help everyone else?

Fallon walked with me back to the tower in the middle of nowhere. Guards stood protecting the doorway, and I told the scribe we were heading back to Earth to fetch the rest of the Fae. A small lie that had caused him to frown but relent since every Fae was welcome here. And we needed every Fae more so now than ever. Perhaps others in the Summer Court would find their fated mates with the Fae living on Earth.

But would that matter if we didn't heal the spring?

Of course it did, everyone deserved to find their fated mate even if they only had them for a short time.

My accompanying guards, Brogan, and Conlan, joined us once again for the trek back to Earth. We stepped inside the tower. The Veil surged like a vortex of wild power. Using my powers, I softened the curtain and readied it for our departure. It seemed the Veil didn't like to be contained as much as us. As we stepped inside, the swirling purple mist intensified, preparing us for our departure back to Earth. We stepped free into the exact location we'd left. The center of Fallon's camp.

Except the camp was no longer here. No caravans made the cozy atmosphere of the place. No Fae either.

"Dammit, they left," Fallon ground out through a tight jaw.

"Without you?"

How could they leave without him? And his sister? Or had she left with the troupe?

"Looks that way." He kicked a stone sending it hurtling across the grassy expanse of the clearing and into the woods.

"Where did they go?"

"They'll be heading to Ireland."

Every muscle in my body stiffened to the point of discomfort.

Not there. Anywhere but where I almost died.

Where I'd lost family members. Where I'd found and lost my fated mate for years. The place wasn't where I wanted to go. Anywhere but there.

"Aislinn?" Fallon dipped his head, so he could look me square in the eyes.

"What about your sister?"

"We'll check Rory's house first, if she's not there, then she must have left with Hamish and the others."

Brogan and Conan folded their arms as though ready to forbid me.

I placed my hand in Fallon's. "We'll find her. I'd hate to imagine my sister or brother missing."

Brogan and Conan exchanged a glance. Since they were brothers, I assumed they felt the same way, and they'd search everywhere for their siblings too.

"They took the car too," Fallon said. "We'll have to walk."

"If you haven't noticed, we walk everywhere."

Fallon's lips pulled into a small smile. "Now that you mention it, have you ever been inside a car? Or train? Or a plane?"

I shook my head. "I travel through the Veil. Much quicker than anything humans might come up with."

"I never traveled through the Veil until today. It's very different to what I imagined. It's almost calm inside it like the eye of a storm."

"You'd appreciate all about storms since you can create them."

"Lightning, not entire storms. Although with the pair of us using our powers, I think we'd be able to make storms."

"Perhaps," I said. "Why would we want to make storms, anyway?"

"Fun?" he winked.

I laughed. "Your idea of fun is strange."

"I don't know. We had fun last night in the storm."

My cheeks warmed remembering the fun I had showing Fallon what it was like to receive oral sex for the first time. My blood heated with the desire to show him more firsts.

"At least he doesn't live in the city," Fallon said setting off along the dirt road. "Might be hard to keep you hidden if he was."

I touched a hand to my flower crown. Over the years it had grown harder for me to be on Earth without my appearance causing questions amongst humans. But then I'd kept to myself as much as possible while looking for a cure to the spring's problems. Perhaps that's why I'd found nothing. If I talked to Fallon about it now, would he know anything since he'd been on Earth all these years?

Then the guards would overhear, and they were the biggest gossips in the Fae Kingdom.

Best to wait until we were alone.

We traipsed along the dirt road for hours. A gray drizzly misty rain fell on us, but it was more of an annoyance than a hindrance. Besides, we didn't suffer from the cold, so the weather didn't bother us.

"It's funny, but I miss the warmth of the Summer Court already," Fallon said.

Brogan and Conlan chuckled.

"The place soothed my powers. Is that what you experience all the time?" he asked.

"I suppose."

I hadn't given my powers much reflection over the years except for when I crossed through the Veil.

"Aye," Brogan said. "Here on Earth, they seem to want free more."

"Interesting." Fallon tapped his finger on his chin. "I wonder why."

"My brother's mate, Sophia, says the Earth's vibrations are off balance now. Perhaps that's what you're sensing?"

"How does she sense vibrations?"

"She's a jaguar shifter. It's part of her powers."

"I've never met a jaguar shifter. Never heard of them either. They must be rare."

"Almost as rare as Fae," I said.

"What does she think is causing the disturbance?"

"She doesn't know, but she believes us Fae can cure the Earth with our powers."

"Makes sense," he said. "Our powers are elemental. If enough of us channeled our powers at once into the planet, then we'd reset it."

"You make it sound simple."

"Nothing is simple. It would require a lot of power. Most likely only royal powers would make a change that enormous."

"Great," I mumbled. "So now amongst everything else, we're supposed to cure this realm?"

"What else is there?" Fallon's sharp gaze hit the side of my face.

My powers throbbed in my palms. Perhaps it was my subconscious making them flare. Maybe it was my mate's presence. Or maybe it was the disturbance in this realm. Whatever it was, I didn't like not being in control.

I was always in control.

"Are we almost there?" I asked, pointing at a house in the distance.

Its windows were alight with a golden glow in the gloomy weather. Welcoming beacons to our wandering. I missed the sunshine of the Summer Court too. The country house of brown bricks and a terracotta tiled roof sat on the grassy hillside. Behind it, trees rose into the sky giving it a backdrop that welcomed Fae. If his sister was here, I understood why she liked the place. There was an earthy, natural atmosphere in the house.

"Princess, let us secure the premises first," Brogan said.

Fallon held my hand as I was about to disagree. "We'll wait here."

I suppose if he was waiting with me, then it wasn't as though I was the weak one. I was stronger than them all. My power would obliterate theirs in its strength. The guards walked toward the house leaving me with Fallon in the drizzling rain and the fading daylight. Moments passed and then they returned looking more embarrassed than I'd ever seen guards look.

"All is safe inside. You may proceed," Brogan said.

"We'll stand guard outside," Conlan said.

Fallon and I walked toward the wooden door, which opened on our approach. His sister stood on the doorstep, arms crossed over her chest, and a very displeased expression on her face.

"Way to ruin the mood," Erin said.

"Did you even realize the troupe has left? That I left?" Fallon said.

"What?" Erin's face drained of color. "Where did you go?"

"If you'd stayed around, you would have known I traveled to the Summer Court."

"Oh." She peered at her feet. "How was it?"

"Fine," he snapped. "What are you doing, Erin? You can't stay here."

"Come inside. Both of you." She stepped back. "We need to talk."

"We will, but not here in front of Rory."

"Rory knows."

"Knows what?" Fallon snapped, his patience wearing thin with his sister.

"He knows what I am." She lifted her head and met her brother's hard glare. "He accepts me for me."

I sucked in a startled breath. A human knowing about Fae. Was that wise? Fallon must have had the same thoughts as me because he said, "What have you done?"

Stepping beside Fallon, I placed a reassuring hand on his back. "Let's go inside and hear what your sister has to say."

Fallon scowled but stepped inside the house. The interior was aglow with the soft golden radiance of the lights we'd spotted over the distance. Warmth filled the room. Erin motioned toward the floral sofa. I urged Fallon toward the seating, and we sat as close as possible without sitting on each other. Rory rushed into the room, a tray in his hands full of steaming mugs.

His hands shook as he passed the tray around and we all collected a mug fast, so the contents didn't spill. I sniffed the cup, smelling only tea, I sipped the warm liquid trying not to grimace at the bitter taste assaulting my tongue. Did he not sweeten it at all? Fae had a sweet tooth for beverages and food. He wasn't supposed to know we existed so I could forgive him for not sweetening the tea.

As soon as he placed the tray on the coffee table, Erin dragged him to sit beside her on the other floral couch.

"So, um, I love your sister," Rory said, not even meeting our faces with his gaze.

The poor young man was so out of his depth that I couldn't stop feeling sorry for him. Here he was in a room with powerful Fae admitting his love for one. It couldn't be easy for him as a human.

Fallon's fingernails tapped on the side of the mug. He'd yet to drink from the cup.

"I love Rory too," Erin said.

Fallon cocked an eyebrow. "I've heard this before."

Erin shook her head wildly. "Not like this."

"Erin." Fallon sighed. "You understand this won't end well. He's—"

"Human," Rory said. "I'm aware I'm mortal and Erin isn't, but I'll love her for as long as she wants me. I live out here away from others. No one will even realize."

"Rory, it doesn't work like that. There is always someone who notices. Why do you think we move so often? I can't allow you to stay here Erin. As your brother and only family, I must protect you."

"Then Rory is coming with us," Erin said standing and placing her hands on her hips.

Fallon shook his head.

"Perhaps he can travel with us," I said, breaking into the conversation before Fallon pushed his sister away even more. I spotted the stubborn tilt of her chin and the way her eyes flashed. The same expression flitted over my sister's face. Sometimes it was easier to go with their stubborn claim and watch it fizzle out rather than go against it. "If he knows about us, then it would be wiser for him to stay close so we can keep an eye on him, anyway."

Besides, if the spring stopped running then we'd become mortal. Erin would be mortal like the man she said she loved. I would never stand between love.

"I wouldn't say anything to anyone," Rory said. "Besides, no one would believe me, anyway. I'd end up locked in a mental hospital."

Frowning, I said, "I do not understand what you're talking about."

"I do," Fallon said with an amused grin across his face. "I'll explain it later."

He lifted the mug to his lips and drank, then spat the liquid back into the cup.

"What is this?"

"Tea," Rory said.

"This is a poor excuse for tea," Fallon said. "Erin, how do you drink this?"

"She loves my tea," Rory said defensively.

Fallon gathered all our mugs and put them back on the tray on the table. "Dia, you must love him to drink this."

"I do," Erin said.

"You don't like my tea?" Rory turned toward Erin.

"Sorry, no, it's not sweet enough."

"Why didn't you say anything?"

Erin's cheeks blushed a pretty shade of pink. "I didn't want to hurt you."

Fallon groaned. "All right. If we leave for the night and come back tomorrow, will you still be here? Or will you run off again?"

Erin glanced away.

"Like I thought." Fallon settled back on the sofa. "Erin, make us some better tea since we're staying here the night, then tomorrow we'll all head to the train station and follow the troupe to Ireland."

Panic shot through my veins. Ireland. Where it all began in a fiery blaze of agony and suffering.

# CHAPTER SEVENTEEN
# FALLON

I RECOGNIZED MY MISTAKE as soon as the words left my mouth. Aislinn couldn't go on a train. She had no form of identification and with the way she looked, the authorities would stop her and ask questions. We didn't need that sort of interest in us. Not that the humans believed in magic anymore. The fact Rory appeared to have taken to Erin's news she was Fae made me question if he already distinguished all the hidden supernatural creatures in the world.

I flung my arm along the back of the sofa behind Aislinn's back and twirled my fingers around the thick braid of her hair. The silky strands soothed me. I wanted more answers before we took Rory anywhere with us.

"So, Rory, you don't seem fazed that we're Fae."

His gaze met mine before ducking to Erin. "I noticed a few things that didn't add up." He shrugged. "I'm a curious person by nature and love reading. The library was helpful." He laughed. "Remember that famous vampire book where the girl finds a book about vampires and understands the guy is one. It was like that."

"There are books about Fae?" Aislinn asked.

"There are books about everything you can ever imagine." He gave Erin a loving smile. "I wasn't one hundred percent sure what she was, but I realized she was magical. I mean, look at her. She's so gorgeous, how could she not be?"

Did I sound like this lovesick fool? Probably. No wonder Hamish and the others had left. I owed them an apology no doubt.

"Most people would freak out though," I shoved on, not convinced Rory was as innocent as he played.

He puffed out a breath through his cheeks. "I freaked out when I saw lightning spark from your hands."

"What?" I scowled. "When did you see that?"

I was always so careful to release my power when there were no humans around. How had Rory snuck up on me? How had he seen me use my power and not say anything? To what end had he kept quiet? Did he want to blackmail me? Or use us?

Rory rubbed the back of his neck. "I... um... followed you one night back to your camp."

"How?"

Hamish was always so careful when driving back to our secluded camp site, Rory shouldn't have been able to follow us. He should never have seen me use my power.

"My uncle, he... ah... he's a pickpocket and a talented thief. He raised me when my parents died in a car crash. The black sheep of the family as they say who I'd never met until the day I went to live with him as a moody teenage boy. He believed teaching me all the tricks of his trade was the best way to communicate with me."

"You're an orphan?"

Damn, I didn't want to sympathize with this young man, but hearing those words did just that. I understood all too well what it was like to lose both parents at once. To be left alone in a world you no longer understood.

"Yes. My uncle is gone now too."

"Just you?" Aislinn asked since my mind had traveled back to that sad time and dumped me into the pits of grief once more.

Rory nodded.

"I'm sorry," Aislinn said. "I can't imagine how that is." She reached across the small coffee table and clasped his hand in hers. Her palms flared for an instant and Rory's eyes widened. What was her power? Was there a unique quality to Aislinn's power as there was in her mother's power? Could she sing to soothe people?

"That's why Erin means the world to me. I'd do anything for her."

Aislinn sat back and once again my fingers found the soft strands of her hair in the braid. Touching my mate grounded me. Made me whole.

"You're willing to leave everything you have here? Move multiple times throughout your mortal life. Age when Erin won't?"

"We talked about the aging thing and neither of us have a problem with it," Rory said.

"Look," Erin said. "You realize how old we are, how long it might take to find a fated mate." She shot a pointed look at Aislinn. "Why can't I choose to be happy for now instead of miserable like you were for hundreds of years?"

Aislinn's too-observant gaze hit the side of my face. Did it only now occur to her that I'd been as miserable without my mate as she'd been without me?

"She's right," Aislinn said. "They both are. If they're happy then that's all that matters."

"Fine," I relented. "Are you ready to experience magic?"

"Erin has shown me her powers over the clouds in the sky. I love the way she can move them."

"Yours and Erin's powers are associated," Aislinn said.

I faced my mate. "Yes, we can use them together if we wish."

"I'm sure that makes for an interesting storm."

I chuckled. "It can be fun."

Her eyes sparkled with interest, but she squashed it as soon as it flared into her mind. Her expressions were so telling now I'd studied them.

"We need to use the Veil to travel to Ireland."

She flinched. Barely noticeable except to me.

"Why?"

"You, and not to mention, your guards won't be able to travel by human means until we acquire fake identification for you and since Hamish is the one that makes them, we won't be able to get them until we meet up with him."

"A human won't be able to go into the Veil." She folded her arms over her chest.

"Shit." I rubbed my forehead. "What do we do then?"

"Rory and I will go by train. The rest of you can go through the Veil," Erin said.

"You want me to trust you to meet us there?" I crossed my arms over my chest too.

"There's no reason for me to stay here," Rory said. "And I have no reason to keep Erin from her family. I see how much she loves you."

"I do," Erin said. "I want us to be a family still even if you don't approve of my relationship."

Sighing, I said, "It's not that I don't approve..."

"What then?"

"I want you to wait for your fated mate."

"Why?"

"Because there is no better affection in the world. You might love Rory, but the way you'll feel for your fated mate will make every other emotion fade into existence by comparison."

Aislinn unfolded her arms as the tension left her body. Little by little my words and actions were getting through to her. I couldn't wait until she believed in me. In us.

"What about your caravan?" Erin asked, changing the subject so dramatically that I recognized my words had meant something to her too.

"Hamish took them all. They're probably on a ferry on their way to Ireland as we speak."

"He is upset with you," Erin said.

"I know."

"Why is he upset?" Aislinn asked.

"About us." My lips firmed into a tight line. I didn't want to upset my mate, but I wouldn't keep the truth from her.

"Whatever for?"

"We've been alone a long time looking out for each other. He thinks I'm selling them out by returning to the Summer Court."

"Selling them out to who?"

"The King."

After seeing the King that was the furthest thing from existence. The King was a tormented man. I understood torment well. The way we beat ourselves up with our own choices. What Hamish didn't understand, since he'd been younger than me at the time of the Trappers, was being back under the King's rule wasn't selling out.

It was a homecoming.

# CHAPTER EIGHTEEN
## AISLINN

F ALLON'S WORDS CONFUSED ME. How was returning to the Summer Court selling out? No one was paying anyone to return.

"The choice is theirs, but my father wanted all Fae to learn about the doorway."

Father may have made questionable choices over the years, but he did everything with the love for his mate, his children, and his people in his mind. There was no way he'd jeopardize anyone.

"Actions speak louder than words," Fallon said.

He was right. I was holding his actions accountable. His words weren't enough for me to trust him. Give him my heart without worrying he'd break it again.

Leave me again.

Understanding lit his eyes as I stared deeply into them.

"Let's go," he said, standing and holding out his hand. "The sooner we get there, the sooner I can talk to Hamish and set things right."

I stood, ignoring his outstretched hand, and I turned to Erin and Rory.

"We'll see you soon."

"Yes." Erin jumped to her feet and gave me a brief hug.

I was so surprised by her show of affection that I stood still not embracing her back. It was more awkward than it should have been. She would be a part of my family once Fallon and I exchanged mating marks.

*Once?*

Since when did it change from considering doing it, to when we would do it?

The man had me in a state of knots. In his presence, I sensed our connection. The need pulsing from my power to mark him as mine. How much free will did fated mates have?

We stepped outside leaving Rory to pack whatever belongings he wanted to take with him as he wouldn't be coming back for many years, if ever. The guards met us at the edge of the garden where the dark shadows of night flittered amongst the trees behind the house. We told them the plan, but they were against it, and said we needed to head back to the Summer Court so the scribe would note our new destination.

I threw my hands up in the air. When the Veil was still locked, it had been so much easier to travel. Even Fallon agreed with them. I could see their point, but I argued with them that we were powerful together and no one more so than me with the royal powers in my body.

A dark shadow flitted behind Fallon. I stopped talking. Fallon frowned. Nothing moved again. I shook my head. I must have imagined it.

Brogan argued we needed to go to the Summer Court.

Leaves rustled.

A twig snapped.

Dark shadows loomed long and large behind Fallon. I opened my mouth to warn him, but a large muscular man stepped behind Fallon and grabbed him from behind pressing a gun to his temple. Two men dressed in dark shirts and black pants joined him, in their hands covered with tattoos were guns aimed at our heads. We'd been too busy arguing to notice them stalking us.

"Don't hurt her," Fallon said, fear making his voice come out less certain.

The guards swarmed in front of me, protecting me from the threat even though they'd left their swords back at Pepper and Lorcan's cottage. They still had their powers as I did. I also had my daggers, but bullets were more damaging than blades and with the decline of the Spring of Life, should I risk Fallon being shot in the head? Let alone my guards or myself.

"We don't want to hurt anyone," one man with a gun said. "The boss wants to talk to you that's all. There's a fight on tonight he needs you to win."

"Funny you need to take me there at gunpoint." Fallon glared at the men.

They shrugged like using guns wasn't a problem or a big deal.

"And your boss is?" Fallon asked.

"Adam Terrence."

Fallon's face paled. Who was this man that worried Fallon? My fingers met the hilt of my daggers behind the backs of the guards. No one detected my movements as I drew the daggers free.

"Why does he want to talk to me?"

"He learned you're leaving. You're his best fighter. He has an offer for you."

"Let me guess," Fallon said. "I keep fighting and he doesn't kill anyone?"

"Something like that," the man said.

My eyes narrowed. Who assumed they'd kill me or Fallon, or even anyone Fallon cared about? I'd murder them all before they hurt us. My powers flared to my palms.

"Aislinn, don't," Fallon said, the warning clear in his words that our powers needed to remain a secret.

My hands shook as I called my powers back. These men couldn't find out about our powers. But more than that, what if they injured us with their bullets and we didn't heal? If Fallon believed I'd let these men take him without a fight, then he was mistaken.

Brogan gawked at me over his shoulder and shook his head. He agreed with Fallon for some stupid reason. We possessed enough power to take control of this situation, but they didn't want to use their powers either. If they'd had their swords strapped to their backs, would they have used them instead? Pity they'd left them in Lorcan's and Pepper's cottage.

"I'll go talk to him," Fallon said.

"No," I yelled.

"Aislinn, my love, I'll be back. I promise."

I stepped to the side to get to Fallon. Brogan followed me as we ducked back and forth a few times in a macabre dance. I was determined to get to my mate. He was determined to protect me.

"Listen to your man," the stranger said. "We don't want to hurt anyone, but we will if we need to."

Every cell in my body vibrated with anger. Power so fierce it throbbed like it was going to explode. I shoved my daggers back into the holsters ready to unleash the extent of my powers and end these men.

Fallon shook his head ever so slightly.

"We'll bring him back soon," the man said. "So long as he and you all cooperate, and he wins his fight."

"See," Fallon said. "I'll be fine. Back in no time at all."

The men backed up toward the trees, deeper into the shadows dragging a half-willing Fallon with them and keeping their guns pointed at us. Fallon's gaze on my face only left when he could no longer do so. The men turned him and shoved him into a car. Lights flickered to life. The motor rumbled. Tires turned, and the car drove away taking Fallon with them.

They'd taken my mate.

I would not let this happen.

No one would harm my mate. Not these men with guns who didn't comprehend our powers. Not their boss who assumed he'd threaten people into doing his bidding. I'd seen the destruction guns and bullets could cause. Rian's mate Sophia was almost killed because of a bullet since she's a jaguar shifter and can die from a fatal wound to the heart. Now our immortality was in question, would a bullet end us too? Or would we make it back to the spring in time for it to heal us?

"Let's follow them."

"How?" Brogan asked. "They're quicker than us in that contraption."

"We'll find them."

"How?" he asked again. "Have you marked him? Can you track him through your mating mark?"

Panic swirled low in my stomach making it heave to the point I contemplated I'd be sick.

"No," I said regretting that decision now.

"Then how?" Brogan asked. "Best we wait here."

"I'm not waiting here to see if they'll even bring him back."

"You're not going anywhere, Princess, except back to the Summer Court," Conlan said.

"No." Power flared to my hands.

"We're your guards. It's not safe here for you right now, so back we go," he said.

"You can't make me," I said childishly.

Conlan parted the Veil. "I can and I will."

I backed away as they stepped forward. There was no way they'd get me to leave without Fallon. As much as I'd denied our connection, he was my fated mate. I wouldn't lose him again. Power surged to my hands so hard and fast it made my head spin with the velocity, the strength in my magic. Years and years of pent-up power surged into a life force of their own.

I let it all go as I threw my head back and screamed at the night sky.

The power.

The pain.

The long years of longing.

I wouldn't let anything stand between us. Even my guards.

The wind blew so forcefully that it launched them backward into the sky. Their bodies hurtled through the air until they became specks. I lowered them to the ground way gentler than I was feeling at that moment. With them too far away to stop me, I marched to the door of the house and knocked.

Rory opened the door. He stared over my shoulder and seeing nothing his eyebrows rose.

"I need to learn where they hold the underground fighting."

"Why?"

"Because they took Fallon there to fight."

"Who took Fallon?" Rory asked.

"Someone named Adam Terrence."

"Fuck," he said.

"What's wrong?" Erin rushed toward the door.

"They took your brother to fight."

"Taken or went to fight?" She frowned, confusion etched across her face.

"Taken. Now tell me where I can find him so I can rescue him."

# CHAPTER NINETEEN
## FALLON

I STOOD IN THE change rooms of the underground fight club, listening to the muffled chants of the crowd. The atmosphere was a lot different when I didn't want to be here. They'd forced me to be here. Torn away from my mate again. And I'd gone without a fight.

I'd known if Aislinn, her guards, or I had used our powers to subdue the goons, then it would have been worse for us. Adam Terrence was the leading crime lord in England. Everyone feared him and for good reason. If I'd known he was the boss of the fighting ring, then I would never have joined that one. There were many others hidden in the world. One just had to recognize where to look, and I'd had enough years of experience to know.

The atmosphere in the room was heavy with the scent of sweat and blood. Desperation. The scent was unfamiliar to me, but I recognized it now I was experiencing it too. I was desperate to get back to Aislinn. Desperate to keep my promise to her.

I wouldn't let her down.

I'd win this fight and then I'd leave. The crime lord would never find us we were that good at disappearing.

The goon who'd spoken outside Rory's house stood guard beside me. He hadn't bothered to hide the gun that was strapped to his side by wearing a jacket and it was plain for everyone to see. He was one of the regular bouncers of the place so him being armed wasn't out of line. This time though, the gun was for me. A way to keep me in line.

They didn't comprehend a bullet wouldn't kill me. It'd hurt, but I'd heal. Not as fast as I once could, but I'd be fine. They could never see that.

Nor the lightning power I wielded from my hands.

So I'd fight. Win. Then go back for Aislinn. Leave the country without a trace and be done with this life. I might even stay in the Summer Court forever where there were no evil humans willing to exploit others.

No wonder the Fae King had sealed the Veil.

I hated him less and less each moment I spent with my mate.

Understood his actions more and more each day too.

I strapped my knuckles with the white tape then flexed them testing the tightness and the flexibility of my hands.

"You've gotta win," the goon said.

"I always win," I reminded him.

"I've seen cockier guys than you lose." He shrugged. "Boss has a lot riding on tonight. It pissed him off when he heard you were leaving and didn't intend to show up tonight."

"Who told him that?"

His beady eyes met mine, but he didn't say a name. Who could it be? Only our troupe knew we were leaving. And Rory. Was he the one? He'd been here to the fights often enough over the last few months. It must have been him.

"It was Rory, wasn't it?"

He shrugged.

"You touch my sister and I'll kill you."

He snorted.

"She's a fine piece of ass."

I stood, flexing my knuckles.

"Although that other woman you were with is more my type."

A deep warning growl rumbled out of my throat. "You touch her, and I'll make you hurt in ways you don't realize exist before I kill you."

He scoffed. "Big talk from a fighter who throws a couple of punches. I'm way more experienced than you in torture. I'm kind of hoping you lose tonight so I can have a crack at all of you."

"Fuck you." I spat on his shoes.

His hand sprang for his gun. The door flung open, and the other goon strode into the room.

"For fuck's sake, Kenny, keep your shit together," the other goon said.

Kenny flipped him the bird.

"Fight time," the second goon said.

I stepped toward him but kept my gaze glued to Kenny's face. The sooner we all left the better. I sensed Kenny wouldn't care if I won or lost when it concerned my sister or Aislinn, and I'd never let him near either of them.

The changing room door opened, and I stepped into the gloomy interior of the hallway leading to the fighting pit. The walk had never felt this long. Every muscle in my body tightened The other fighter was already in the ring winding the crowd up by prowling around the ropes and waving his meaty fists in the air. The guy was an ass. I'd seen him fight others, but I hadn't had the pleasure of beating him yet. As soon as the crowd spotted me walking out of the hallway, they became wild cheering my fighter's name instead of his.

"Fuse," they screamed.

Seemed like many people had money on me tonight. I was up against the next-best fighter. Iron Claw, who prowled around the ring like a caged tiger. He'd covered his fists in gray tape adding to his name. He might have an excellent reputation as a fighter, but no one in many, many years had beaten me.

I wouldn't lose.

As cocky as that sounded there was more riding on this than my ego. There was Aislinn. I'd promised her I'd be back, and I would be. Nothing and no one would keep me from my mate. This short period away from her was killing me she wasn't by my side, but I couldn't risk any harm coming to Aislinn. This was the best and quickest outcome to the problem. Win the fight then disappear.

I circled the man and waited for the bell to ring.

From the corner of my eye, I glimpsed the attendant lift his hand to ring the bell. I stepped forward, ready to land the first punch. The bell rang and my fist was already on the way toward Iron Claw's face. It landed in a bone-crunching blow that reverberated up my arm. Iron Claw's head flew backward. He staggered on his feet but righted himself and with a look of pure wrath, he launched himself at me.

He swung with his right, but the blow was a fake and lured me into his left hand which was already swinging upward. His fist grazed the edge of my chin and lip, splitting my lip open and sending blood flying through the air. I shook it off and rounded on him. We exchanged blows for the next minute until he tired. I didn't. I could take blows as well as I gave them. There was always a cathartic sensation about being hit. As though I deserved the pain, but today I didn't experience that.

Today the hits just made me angry.

I hated being here.

Hated being away from Aislinn.

I never wanted to be in a fight again.

I swung with every ounce of strength in my immortal body felling my opponent with one hit, but I'd already followed through with my other fist, and that too caught him in the face smashing his nose so hard bones cracked and blood spurted over both of us. His body landed on the mat in a thud of unconscious weight.

The crowd jumped to their feet and cheered. The ringing of clapping echoed in my ears. I'd made many people money with that knockout in the first round. Sometimes I let the rounds go to two or three before showing my opponent I was toying with them, but today I was too anxious to get back to Aislinn.

Too worried she'd leave me and head back to the Summer Court.

Too scared I'd be separated from her for years on end again.

Maybe Hamish was right in his thinking I put her before the troupe. There had to be a balance. A way for everyone to be happy.

The ring announcer lifted my hand in the air. The crowd cheered again as we turned to every corner of the dingy room. A man dressed in an immaculate suit lifted his glass and tipped it my way.

*Was that the boss?*

I strained to keep my eyes on him, but the ring announcer turned me to the next side and when I spun back the man was no longer in the crowd. As he lowered my arm, I shook him off and strode for the exit. The goon stepped by my side as I walked back to the changing room and flung open the door.

I shrugged on my clothes over my sweat-dampened skin. Unease skittered down my spine that the goon was still here even though I'd won the fight.

The door flung open and the man who'd tipped his drink at me entered with the other goon at his side.

"Boss," the goon inside the change room said.

"You said I could leave after the fight." I curled my fingers into fists.

"Did I?" Terrence Adams said. "I don't recall talking to you before now."

My power wanted to fry him on the spot. Maybe that would solve this growing problem before me.

"Now," Terrence Adams said. "I own you. You fight here for me. There will be no running off not when you earn the most money around here."

"No one owns me," I seethed.

He chuckled darkly. "I do now unless you want me to chain that sweet little sister of yours up in a dungeon." He pointed a finger at my chest. "Don't cross me. I have the means to make everyone you care about suffer."

And then the door flew open again and Aislinn stood in the doorway.

# CHAPTER TWENTY
# AISLINN

WE'D MADE IT TO the underground ring in time to watch Fallon fight. The sheer power behind each punch was clear to see. The way his arm muscles flexed under the lights before each strike made me realize how much care he'd taken with me. Veins throbbed in his forearms and wrapped around his muscular biceps. A light sheen of sweat made his skin glisten. If I wasn't already attracted to Fallon, then I would be now after that masculine display of power. There was something to be said about a man who would fight for what he believed in. Fallon believed in us.

It was time I did too.

I'd heard the man's words through the door. I'd sensed the emotions in them too. The intent was to do Fallon great harm and those he loved. We'd suffered enough and no one would ever make us experience torture again. I closed the door behind me flicking the lock in place.

"Fallon, you were magnificent," I said, with every pair of eyes on me.

The men who'd taken Fallon raised their eyebrows at me as though they couldn't believe I'd made it here for the fight.

"Who are you?" the man in a suit said.

"I'm Fallon's... partner," I said instead of using the word 'mate'. These humans wouldn't understand the enormity of the word. "We're getting married soon, isn't that right, honey?"

Fallon stared at me like I'd lost my mind, but he recovered before the men's eyes landed on him.

"Yes," Fallon said.

"It's why we were going away for a bit." I flicked my hair over my shoulder. "My family has a big ceremony planned back home."

"Well, I guess congratulations are in order," the man said. "Why didn't you say anything?"

"I... ah..." Fallon babbled at a loss for words.

"It's rather sudden." I stepped closer to the suited man.

"Oh, you're pregnant." His eyes glittered with glee, but the emotions in his words sent shivers up my spine. He'd use anyone Fallon loved against him, even a pretend unborn child.

Fallon choked on his saliva.

"Shh." I tapped a finger to the man's lips. "It's a secret. My family wants us to be married first. You can see why we must rush. When your men fetched Fallon for the fight, I worried we wouldn't make the train and we'd miss the wedding."

I fluttered my eyelashes at the man putting on a show for his benefit rather than stabbing him like I wanted to. I still may do just that.

The man touched my flower crown. "Is that why you have flowers in your hair? For the wedding?"

Iciness weaved through my body with his words and his touch.

"Aye. I mean yes. Do you like them?" I asked instead of slicing off his hand for daring to touch me. I couldn't strike until Fallon was away from the goon at his side. I wouldn't risk him getting hurt.

The suited man spun around no longer facing me and giving me the target of his back. Much easier to slip a knife into his heart now. Although the guards would be harder to take out. One was too close to Fallon that if I made an advance now, he'd hurt Fallon, and I wouldn't let that happen. At least the other one was far enough away that once I threw my daggers, he'd fall without harm to either of us.

"I never pegged you for the marrying type," he said to Fallon.

"Yeah, well, I figured I should do the right thing after knocking her up," he said falling into my act now. "She's a bit of an airhead and needs looking after."

Dia, that hurt even though he was trying to get us out of here without violence where I might get hurt. His protectiveness warmed my heart, but I could take care of myself. I'd trained every day for centuries. There was no way a human would get the best of me again and these men here wouldn't even have the chance to try.

They'd all be dead soon.

"You're even better collateral," the leader said.

His words proved the vibrations hanging in the air. These people would do anything to use Fallon.

The man closest to Fallon laughed. Fallon sidled away from him while my over-the-top acting distracted him. That was all I needed to act. I slipped two daggers free, slid one through the ribs of the suited man into his heart, and flung the other dagger at the man behind Fallon landing the blade in his throat. His arms flung up to his neck as blood gurgled from his mouth. Fallon's eyes widened, and then they darkened with anger. The other man reached for his gun, but Fallon lunged for him and tackled him to the ground before I could get another knife free and thrown in his direction.

Fallon's fists flew one after another. The sound of flesh hitting flesh echoed in my ears until the man underneath Fallon stopped moving. Fallon scrambled to his feet and nudged the man in the side with his foot, but no movement came from him. The rest of the sounds filtered back to me and filled the room with the gurgled noises of men straining to breathe. Struggling to live. The suited man fell to his knees, his head turned over his shoulder, eyes wide with shock stared at me as the life left him and he collapsed onto the floor.

Fallon rushed forward, clasped my hands in his, and said, "Don't look. Look at me."

But I couldn't stop staring at the men I'd killed. I'd slain no one before and as the light left all their eyes and the room fell silent except for mine and Fallon's heavy breathing, the enormity of my actions hit me. My knees wobbled, but Fallon's brawny arms caught me around the waist, and he hauled me against his chest sealing off my view of the dead humans.

The air caught in my lungs. I hauled in a deeper breath but that drew in the metallic tang in the air.

"Let me get you out of here," he said.

I was stronger than this. These men would have hurt us if we hadn't destroyed them.

Yanking out of his arms, I said, "I need my daggers back."

I strode over to each body and withdrew them, wiped the blades clean on their clothes, and then holstered them on my body again.

Fallon cocked his head to the side as he studied me, and said, "Are you okay?"

"Why wouldn't I be?" I asked. "They wanted to hurt you. Would have wounded you if I hadn't intervened."

"How do you recognize that?" he asked unwrapping the bloody tape from his fists.

"My powers."

"What about them?"

"Every word that travels through the air vibrates. My powers control air vibrations so I can sense things in the air that others cannot."

"Such as?"

"Emotions."

"Is that why you don't use them? Because you sense emotions?"

"Aye," I said. "It's tiring."

"I'm sorry."

"What are you sorry for?"

"For all this." He swept his arm around the room. "You murdered them for me. If I hadn't been involved in this life, then you wouldn't have had to."

"'Tis no hardship killing for my mate."

His lips spread into a grin. "You called me your mate."

"Well, that's what you are."

"Let's get rid of these bodies, talk to Hamish and the others, then we can head back to the Summer Court for good."

"You'd leave here for me? You'd leave your sister?"

"I'd do anything for you. You killed those men for me. If you want the moon, then I'd find a way to give it to you."

I closed the distance between us. "Silly mate. The moon belongs in the sky."

He lowered his head and whispered, "It probably disgusts you, but that was a turn-on seeing you throw those daggers."

I rubbed my body against his. "It probably disgusts you that I found you fighting a turn-on too."

He chuckled huskily before closing the distance between our mouths and kissing me passionately. My body ached for him to touch. For him to fill me with his cock. To give me nothing but him and only him. We'd almost been torn apart for the second time.

"I need you," I whispered against his mouth.

"I need you too."

Our lips slammed together again as urgency throbbed through my body. I needed my mate now. He needed me. I tugged down his shorts freeing his hard erection and wrapped it in the warmth of my hand. He groaned sending the vibrations through his lips and tongue. I rolled my hips. His hands tugged at my dress until he gathered the material into his fists at my waist. Then he shifted it into one hand while his other coasted over the bared flesh of my buttocks. My hips rocked against him seeking what only he would give me.

"Spread your legs. Let me give you what you need," he said.

I widened my legs eager for my mate. His hand brushed the sensitive skin of my hip as it drifted toward the front before dipping between my legs. I widened my legs even more and his fingers found my slick, eager flesh. One stroke of his fingers was enough to set the desire out of control. Fingers that had pummeled a man to the ground. Fists that had beat the life out of a man so he wouldn't hurt me. A fresh surge of arousal seeped from me.

"You feel so good. Do you like me touching you?"

"Aye." I rolled my hips toward his hand wanting him to plunge them deep inside.

My grip on his cock tightened as his fingers teased my entrance. The soft strokes around where I needed him most made me pant and moan. Grind my hips trying to force him inside me.

"I need..." I gasped as his finger thrust inside me. "Aye, that."

"Like this?" he asked, pumping his finger inside my tightening core.

"More," I demanded. I needed all of him, but this here would have to do for now since he wanted to wait to have sex until after I'd marked him.

That couldn't come soon enough.

He slid a second finger inside me making me feel fuller, more pleasure as he thrust them in time to the way I pumped my hand up and down his cock. His lips landed back on mine again and we kissed and stroked until the world and its problems fell away. Until there was only us and the way our hands touched each other. The way our mouths caressed over the others.

The pleasure inside me tightened to the point of no return. One more stroke of his fingers and I careened over the edge of the pleasure into the freefall of an orgasm. My feet tensed as I raised on my toes. Deep inside my muscles contracted around his fingers. My hand worked faster on him eager for Fallon to experience this pleasure too. He came with a shuddering breath. His release jetted over my palm and the top of my hand. A shiver ran through his entire body.

He dropped his forehead to mine and rested it there as we both breathed heavily. Both of us didn't want to let go of the other, but we knew we had to. Comprehended we couldn't spend any longer in his changing room with dead bodies around us. We'd survived and proved we'd always survive together. He kissed my forehead, withdrew his fingers, and settled my dress back around my legs.

"You're so beautiful. I can't believe how lucky I am you're my mate."

I stroked him once more, smiling as his cock twitched in my palm before pulling his shorts back up and covering him. Such a shame he kept making us wait.

"Well, mate, how are we going to deal with this?" I swept a hand around the room.

# CHAPTER TWENTY-ONE
## FALLON

"**H**OW DID YOU GET here?"

"Rory and Erin drove me."

I wanted to throttle the pair of them for driving my mate to this place. For putting her in danger.

"And where are your guards?"

"They wanted to take me back to the Summer Court, so I blew them away with my powers. They'll be fine. Perhaps a little annoyed."

"A little?" I scoffed. "They will be pissed off."

Aislinn gave me a small smile as though pissing off her guards made her amused. I drew in a grounding breath but her arousal and my release hung heavy in the metallic-scented air. Death and arousal were a combination I didn't think would go together, but with my mate, anything she did made me want her.

"All right, go get Rory to drive to the back door, pop his trunk and I'll carry them out there."

"By yourself?"

"I'll manage."

I knew how to get these bodies out of here. There were enormous gear bags that would fit their bodies. Hauling them through the dark hallway out the back door while fights were still going was the simple part. Fitting three of them into the trunk of a car would be the hard part.

Aislinn swept a quick kiss to my lips and unlocked the door before slipping through a small gap. I locked it behind her and set to work bagging the bodies. The blood on the floor would have to stay, but there were so many old bloodstains in this building that no one would question it. Well, that was my hope at least. People would miss the crime boss, but as an evil person, he had many enemies. I wouldn't register on the radar as one of them. No one knew about this underground ring except for the fighters and the crowd. Neither of those would get the police involved. No doubt now the boss was dead, this ring would end.

It was a better time than ever to leave.

With the bodies in the enormous bags, I snuck one of them along the dark hallway not encountering a single person which was to be expected at this time of night. I eased open the back door and hefted the bag down the steps. Aislinn stood beside a large truck, her forehead pinched with concern. Her expression made the love inside me grow even quicker.

Rory stood beside her and Erin on his other side. They appeared as concerned as Aislinn, but their worry didn't hit me as hard as Aislinn's.

"Glad you've got a truck," I said.

Rory's eyes widened as I hefted the bag into the back of the truck.

"One down, two to go."

"Shit," Rory said. "I'll help."

Rory followed me back into the building. He'd been a regular visitor here over the last few months. It was how he'd met Erin. He slid along the hallways like a shadow in the night. I'd never observed his stealth before today, but discovering his history, it made sense he walked swiftly and silently. But was there more to Rory? Was he part of the boss's gang?

The two bags were still on the floor of my changing room where I'd left them against a wall. We grabbed one each and made our way back to Rory's truck. At least he had a truck that was big enough to fit three bodies. I never considered I'd be hefting body bags around and being thankful for a large truck to transport them. My mate had surprised me with her lack of hesitation about killing a threat. Once we returned and stowed the other bodies in the truck, we climbed into the vehicle and Rory drove away from the building.

"Where to?" Erin asked.

She didn't appear upset about the dead bodies either. Dia, the women in my life were strong. Not that I was complaining.

"As far into the countryside as we can get where I can incinerate them."

Rory's fingers tightened on the steering wheel.

"Do you have a problem?" I asked.

"No." Rory's gaze found mine in the rearview mirror. The awe and fear mingling in his eyes made me wonder if he felt that way from the deaths or my powers. We drove in silence for hours. Aislinn stared out the window. Erin sat close to Rory, and I had no clue what to say.

"Here will do," I said and tapped his shoulder. "Head over that hill."

Rory drove over the hill and headed into the dip, stopping the truck at the bottom. I jumped out and hauled the first body bag from the back of the truck onto the grassy green earth. Rory joined me and helped with the next body, and we piled it on top of the next one. Aislinn and Erin exited the truck, but they didn't help or offer to help with moving the bodies. At least my mate was letting me take care of this for her.

When the last body landed on top of the others, I told Rory to drive his truck further away so it wouldn't get damaged. He drove a short distance away and then jogged back.

"We didn't get any fuel to burn them," he said.

"Don't need it." I slapped his shoulder letting a small amount of my powers flare to my hands.

He scampered back to Erin's side, his face whiter than I'd ever seen. I guess that answered my questions if he feared death or my powers.

Erin's face pinched in concentration as her powers surged to her hands. Dark clouds rolled across the night sky blocking out the moon and leaving the threat of a storm on the horizon.

I let go of the tight control of my powers and summoned the electricity. My palms glowed. Sparks shot through the sky and into the ground at my feet straight into the pile of bodies. The silvery purple power surged so hard and fast the bodies glowed and then disintegrated into tiny particles of ash. A fierce breeze blew through the ash sending them scattering across the landscape and erasing all evidence of the bodies.

"Thanks," I said to Aislinn and Erin.

"Now if only we had Saoirse here, she'd be able to produce the rain to go with the storm," Aislinn said.

I stepped closer to Aislinn and threaded my arm around her waist. "I'd like to meet the rest of your family."

"She lives on Earth with her mate." Her petite brows puckered. "But she visits us now."

I sensed there was a story there, but she was so slow in giving me any information I grasped I shouldn't force her until she told me herself. Until she trusted me.

Instead, I focused on Rory and the possibility he might have been working with these men.

"How did they know we were leaving?" I folded my arms over my chest to stop myself from frying Rory on the spot with my powers.

Erin shrugged. Aislinn's eyes landed on my face, and she did the little head tilt she did when she was thinking.

"And how did they know to find us at your house Rory?"

Rory's throat worked hard as he swallowed. Erin swung toward him as though she'd realized I was right to question him.

"Rory?" Erin whispered.

Rory stepped backward. Aislinn had a dagger in her hand so quickly that it was there in less than a second.

"Wait!" Rory cried.

I placed a restraining hand on Aislinn's shoulder.

"I didn't have a choice. They caught me picking pockets at the fight club and threatened to hurt Erin. I couldn't let them hurt her. I love her so much." He threw a pleading gaze at Erin. "I'm sorry. It was the only thing I had to barter your life with."

"They wouldn't have been able to kill me," Erin yelled.

"No, but they would have hurt you and I couldn't have that on my conscience." He placed his palms together as though begging her. "There was one guy there who kept saying..." he gulped. "He'd do awful things to you."

I understood who he was talking about since the goon had said similar things to me about Aislinn and Erin. But still...

"So you told them what?" I asked, barely keeping the rage from my words.

"Nothing. I told them hurting Erin would make them lose their prize fighter, but that they were losing you, anyway." He gulped again. "I wasn't thinking straight, and it slipped out. I didn't mean to tell them anything at all, but you don't understand how brutal they are... or were."

Rory stared at the spot on the ground where I'd incinerated the bodies. Was he wondering if he'd be next?

"What else did you tell them?"

"Nothing, nothing at all," Rory babbled. "I'd never tell anyone who you are or what you can do." He sniffed as though he was about to cry. "I love Erin and I never want to see her hurt in any way."

"You don't think this has hurt me?" Erin asked in a whisper.

"Erin, please, I didn't mean to hurt you. I was scared and out of my mind with worry about what they'd do to you."

"So you put my brother in harm's way?" Erin stepped closer to me. "I don't know if I can forgive you."

"But?"

"But what?" I asked wrapping an arm around Erin's shoulders.

Aislinn stepped around the other side and protected Erin too. I loved her more each moment we spent together. Her protectiveness extended to my family, and it made my chest feel fuller.

Tears hovered on Rory's eyelashes. "Are you going to kill me?"

"Oh, Rory." Erin sighed. "We won't kill you."

"Really?" He blinked the tears back before they streamed down his face.

Erin shook her head. Aislinn let out a sigh as though she thought that was the wrong choice, but this was Erin's choice in the end. I wasn't sure what to think. Rory had been wrong to tell them, but had Erin told him it was a secret, and he shouldn't tell anyone?

"Did Erin tell you us leaving was a secret?" I asked voicing the question in my mind.

"No." He shook his head. "I didn't tell anyone else if that's what you're thinking."

Relief shot through me when he said that, but that wasn't what I'd been thinking.

"I was thinking, you might be more innocent than we're making you out to be."

"How so?" Aislinn asked with another one of her head tilts.

"If he didn't know not to tell people we were leaving, then he didn't know he was revealing a secret, did he? And if he didn't know, and he was simply protecting Erin, then can we fault him?"

Aislinn's eyebrows rose, and she sheathed her dagger.

"I understand the need to protect the one you love."

Our gazes met and held. Erin launched herself at Rory and he caught her in his arms.

"I'm sorry, so sorry," he said, hugging her tight to his body. "I'll never tell anyone anything ever again. I swear it on my life. They can kill me for all I care so long as they never hurt you."

Erin kissed him. I longed to take Aislinn in my arms and kiss her too, but we'd spent enough time out here when we should have been catching up with Hamish and the troupe. Erin and Rory stepped a little away from us and whispered to each other. I supposed they were making up. Aislinn inched closer to me.

"I'm not sure I trust him," she whispered.

"Me either, but he doesn't appear to have done anything wrong. Erin loves him and we'd break her heart if we ended his life. Besides, if he loves her as he says he does, then he'll protect her. If we forced them apart now, who knows what he'd do, or who he'd tell about us."

"I suppose you're right."

Erin and Rory walked back to us arm in arm as though still happy in love. My sister was more forgiving than me. I glanced at Aislinn, I suppose that wasn't right since I'd forgiven Aislinn for stabbing me in the heart with a knife.

"We're heading to the train station now," Erin said. "Rory's worried about all of this coming back to us."

"No one will suspect us."

Rory scrubbed a hand over his face. "No disrespect, but when a mob boss and his men go missing and we do too, who do you think they'll suspect?"

"They won't find a trace of us. Besides, there would be documentation of Hamish and the other's departure before this happened, so we have an alibi."

"How do you figure?" Rory asked.

"He would have booked tickets for Erin and me." I stroked a hand over Aislinn's back. "Aislinn didn't exist here until a short time ago and the only people who would have seen her were the ones at the fight ring. They won't say anything. The only one without an alibi is you."

"Don't think about pinning this on me," Rory said.

It would be one way to deal with Rory and not have his death on our hands, but then Erin would be sad.

"Rory, that's not what he meant," Erin said.

I shrugged. "I was simply stating that Rory has a point. They might suspect him with these disappearances, but no one will recognize you where we're going. Unless you've changed your mind about coming with us?"

Rory glared at me. "I'm staying with Erin no matter what, for as long as she'll have me. I realize I have a lot to grovel for and I will."

My damn sister glowed when he said that. I suppose I had to accept that this was who she wanted even if it made no sense to me. Not when she would one day have a fated mate.

"I don't trust you," I said. "What makes you think I'll let you travel with Erin?"

"I would jump in front of a train for Erin," Rory said. "Whatever it takes to keep her safe, I'll do."

He knew all the right things to say, but it'd be a long time before I ever trusted him.

"I trust Rory," Erin said.

Was she a fool? Or was I a fool to consider letting her travel to Ireland with him? But I would always put my mate first, now and forever.

"We'll see you in Ireland then," I said.

She gave me a small nod as I glanced down at her. The way her eyes lit with understanding and reassurance made me pause.

Aislinn stepped forward and handed Erin a dagger. "Use this if you need to."

Erin stared at the dagger in her palm but pressed it back in Aislinn's hand.

"I won't need it. Besides, I can't carry a weapon on the train. I have my powers, and I learned self-defense moves one year. When was that?"

I shrugged trying to recall the year she'd frequented the gym I'd trained at taking self-defense classes because of the instructor who she'd fallen for. A human too. That hadn't lasted long. Maybe I was worried for no reason about Rory, and this would be over before too long too. Then we'd have to worry about what to do with him and his knowledge.

"Quite a few years ago now," I said.

"Thank you though, Aislinn." Erin hugged my mate.

Aislinn's arms squeezed her back quickly. "Stay safe."

Rory helped Erin into his truck and then drove away leaving us standing in the middle of nowhere, but that didn't matter when we'd use the Veil to travel.

"I'm worried," Aislinn said.

"As am I, but she's a grown woman. She has power and skills." I clasped her hand in mine. "But you will always come first."

Aislinn's lips turned up into a small smile. "I doubt very much your sister would be helpless with a brother like you."

"I may have shown her a few things over the years," I said, smirking.

"See she'll be fine, but we can worry together."

I grinned. She was right.

Aislinn lifted her hand and called on the Veil. Her power and beauty astounded me but even more so when she used her powers.

"What about your guards? Shouldn't we go back and get them?"

She smiled seductively at me. "How about a bit of alone time first?"

# CHAPTER TWENTY-TWO
## AISLINN

A LONE TIME. TRUE ALONE time, we hadn't had yet. There were always others around us. Other's problems. Our problems. Fallon swooped me into his arms and spun me around as though dancing on a dark hillside after burning evil people's bodies was the best thing to dance to. What would he think of our Fae balls? The singing and dancing? Intricate attire? I wanted to show him it all. Not the fleeting visit we'd had at the Summer Court. I longed to take him home and show him everything that made the Fae Kingdom magical.

Made us magical too.

Waving my hand over the Veil, it parted for my powers. The more I'd used them of late, the easier it was to process the sounds and sentiment behind them coming to me in the air. Easier still with my mate by my side. He centered my powers. Made the vibrations effortless to deal with.

The magic curtain closed around us, and Fallon took the moment to plant a kiss on my lips before nuzzling my hair with his nose.

"I want to undo your braid again. Let all this wild hair free."

"Do it," I said.

He'd put me first before his sister yet again and now I truly believed him when he said he'd put me first always.

His fingers found the ribbon on the end of the thick braid and tugged it loose, tying it around his wrist, he stroked the strands free of the tight braid. Every inch he released his fingers sent tiny shivers dancing over my scalp and down my back. I wanted him so very much it was impossible to deny our connection. Impossible to deny they had fated him to me.

"Where are you taking us?" he whispered in my ear.

"I'm not sure." I laughed.

He placed a hand over my heart. "Where does this want to take us?"

I tipped my head to the side giving his warm lips better access to the soft skin of my neck. He took the invitation and trailed gentle kisses along my neck up to my ear again as he whispered, "Take us home."

"Home is the Summer Court."

"Then let's go there."

"What about Ireland and your troupe?"

"They can wait. We can't wait any longer to claim each other."

I nodded and parted the Veil to home. We stumbled in each other's arms through the Veil into the atrium. I didn't care about going through the tower. About protocol. About guards or anyone else right in this moment, there was only Fallon and me.

His face lit with awe as he gawked around the atrium and the magical heart of the palace. Flowers hung from the open ceiling sending their perfume around the atrium along with the water's fresh smell, the smallest of trickles running from the spring.

"Is this the Spring of Life?"

"Aye."

"Wow." He gaped in further awe at the running water falling from the rocks into the stream below.

"This is your home?"

"Here in the atrium is the place I'm the most at home."

"Then mark me here," he said. "Make me yours, Aislinn."

I chewed on my lip pulling the kiss-ravaged flesh into my mouth. Here was perfect. I couldn't deny us any longer. I trusted he'd always be with me. Stepping closer I laid my hand on his chest.

"Mark me too."

Surprise flitted over his face before he raised his palm to my chest. Our lips met again in a desperate kiss. I let go of my power and let it surge into his chest. Let it mark him as mine. His power flared to his palm and heated my flesh. Images flitted through my mind of him as a young child. Wild and willful he raced through the village. I recognized the place. It was the closest village to my grandparent's farm.

"Aislinn," he rasped my name before falling to the cobblestones under our feet.

I placed a hand on my head as my body swayed. We should have laid down before doing this. My knees crumpled, and I fell beside Fallon landing in a heap while we both slipped into the Quiet to absorb each other's memories. To become joined as mates in the way of the Fae.

The small child ran through the village in my mind. Fallon. He was so adorable as a child. I longed to squeeze his chubby little cheeks in the way my grandmother had with me. Dia, I missed her. I missed all of them. I observed Fallon's parents. They were sweet together. They were so loving toward Fallon and when his little sister was born, he was the best big brother ever. The horrendous night flashed through my mind when the Trappers attacked the village. Fallon was so young. A short time ago he'd turned twenty. Such a young age for a Fae. And his sister was much younger. Old enough to understand she needed to run and hide but not old enough to understand much more.

I hadn't realized.

Hadn't understood the reason he was still a virgin was because he was young.

I was almost two hundred years old when the Trappers destroyed our lives. So much older than Fallon. I sat up with a start and stared into the peaceful face of my mate lying beside me. My fingers itched to trace the contours of the handsome man who was now mine in the most important way. The agony he'd suffered while we'd been apart knowing there was no way to get to me, no way to reassure me he'd tried to get to me. That he wanted me. Would always want me. He'd been in as much anguish as me, except I'd believed he was dead.

"Oh Fallon," I whispered. "Why didn't you say you were so young? I would never have stabbed you in the heart if I'd known."

"Did you just say you stabbed your mate in the heart?" Ciara asked, walking into the atrium, a book tucked under her arm.

I rocked back on my heels and stood.

"Ciara, you're always so sneaky."

She tapped her fingers on the book. "Not my problem if you didn't hear me."

"No one ever hears you." My fingers caressed the hilt of my dagger. Seemed my protectiveness over my mate extended to family members too.

"Don't even think about stabbing me with one of your daggers."

My hand dropped to my side. "Sorry, I guess I'm overprotective of my mate."

She snorted. "Seems a family trait. What's his name?"

"Fallon."

"Does Mother and Father know?"

"No, Father wasn't himself when I last talked with him. How is he now?"

"He didn't attend dinner last night and I haven't seen him today, but it's not usual to go a day without seeing him. He spends a lot of time in his study now."

"What is he doing in there?"

She lifted the book. "He's trying to find a cure for the spring like the rest of us."

"Still no luck?"

She shook her head throwing the long silvery blonde strands of her hair flying. My hand ran through my hair recalling Fallon untying it before we'd come here. I'd meant something different when I'd suggested alone time. More orgasms were on my agenda, but I suppose now we'd marked each other we'd have sex.

So there was that to look forward to when he woke from the Quiet whenever that would be.

But now he'd comprehend about the spring. I let out a long breath. Why couldn't anything be easy?

"We need to find a cure soon." Ciara stared at the dwindling spring. "Time is running out."

"I sense it too."

Fallon groaned. The bruises on his face from the fight were still dark on his skin. Why hadn't he healed yet? Was it the spring? My stomach churned. I should have told him about the spring's problems. I rushed over to the trickle of water and scooped a handful into my palm. Slowly, I lowered it to his cheek and stroked the healing water over his skin. The bruise healed instantly. I let out a sigh of relief. How long had we been in the Quiet? It was so hard to tell when I'd been absorbed in Fallon's memories.

"He's waking already?" Ciara asked.

"It looks that way. I'm surprised since he's so young."

She tapped the book. "He's a Fae though. From what I've read they take our mating mark easier than anyone else. Plus, it depends on the strength of their powers. He must be strong to wake so soon from a Fae royal's mating mark."

"Fallon has endured so much on Earth while we locked him out. He kept all the children in his village safe. Helped them grow and hide their powers as the world changed around them."

"He's a leader." Ciara nodded. "Makes sense."

"What does?"

"That he'd be your mate. Think about it. Every one of the royal's mates has been a leader of some sort."

"I wonder why?"

Ciara opened the book and flicked to a page. "I found a passage in this book about a great change being predicted."

Every muscle in my body tightened. "We already had a great change."

"Maybe this one will make everything better."

"Predictions are for the hopeful."

"Don't you hope we can one day travel without restrictions between the realms like we used to?"

"I'm not sure, Ciara. The Summer Court is safe."

"But there's no excitement."

"You want excitement? How about humans who took your mate and forced him to fight for them? Is that excitement enough for you? Or is me killing them better?"

Ciara's gaze landed on Fallon as he sat up.

"Aislinn, those humans meant nothing," Fallon said, placing a hand on his forehead.

"Nothing? They wanted to keep you as their prize fighter. How's that nothing?"

"It's the way evil humans are."

"Where there are humans there will always be evil." I folded my arms over my chest. "I think Father had the right idea in sealing the Veil."

Ciara rolled her eyes. "So overprotective. We can learn to live in harmony with them again. I know we can."

"You've never even been to Earth," I yelled.

My voice echoed through the atrium. Fallon scrambled to his feet and placed his hands on my shoulders from behind.

"And I want to go," she yelled back. "We should have choices."

She turned on her heel and stomped from the atrium. Fallon's arms wrapped around me from behind. I sagged into his embrace letting my head fall back on his shoulder.

"Sorry. That was my other sister Ciara. Not a great way to meet her."

He dropped a kiss to the top of my head.

"We rarely fight. Everything is falling apart."

"The last few years my power has been more volatile. I always shrugged it off as the fact we hadn't been to our hometown for a while. When I visit the place, it always calms them. But after seeing your memories and the way you keep saying you all are acting off lately too, I'm more inclined to say the spring's problems are affecting every Fae."

"Every Fae?" I twisted my head back to look at Fallon.

"Now I understand about it, yes."

"Shite."

He cupped my face and kept it facing him. "Why didn't you tell me about the problem?"

"We don't want to alarm everyone."

"But I'm your mate. You can trust me with the truth."

His expression looked so hurt that I regretted not telling Fallon and him finding out from my memories.

"I want to," I admitted, and I did. I wanted the love and trust mates shared.

"We'll work on it. We might not have forever now, but we'll make every day matter." He kissed my forehead again.

And in that moment, I experienced the first spark of love for my mate. He'd accepted my flaws. My insecurities, and he hadn't attempted to change me, but was patient in making me see I could trust him.

"Now, how about that alone time you wanted?" he asked.

# CHAPTER TWENTY-THREE
## AISLINN

I WALKED FALLON THROUGH the palace toward my bed chambers with my fingers crossed I didn't come across any of my other siblings. One altercation was one too many. I now understood how my bad mood must have been for them over the last few centuries. I needed to apologize to them. More than ever if we would soon be mortal.

My blood heated with excitement as I opened the door to my bed chambers. The room was as I'd left it, not a thing out of place, messy sheets and all. Fallon walked toward the nearest target with the dagger marks etched in the wood. He traced a finger over them.

"So brutal," he said. "It's hot watching you throw your knives."

I cocked an eyebrow and bit by bit lifted the length of my dress until the dagger at my thigh was in sight. I slid it free and tossed it through the air. The dagger sailed across the room, past Fallon's ear, and embedded in the target.

His nostrils flared. "Hot."

I laughed, and the rest of my daggers followed the first in quick succession forming a silhouette of Fallon on the target.

"How am I so lucky to have you as mine?"

"Stop talking and make love to me."

I shimmied the shoulders of my dress down my arms and let it fall in a pool of silken fabric at my feet.

"Fuck me," he ground through clenched teeth.

"That's the idea."

His fingers curled into fists.

"What's wrong?"

"What if I don't live up to everyone else you've been with?"

I walked toward him and cupped his face in both hands.

"Fallon, you're my mate. Anything you do to me, I promise I'll enjoy. This is different, so much different from when I was with any other man."

He lifted his hands to cover mine on his face as though he didn't want me to let him go.

"You should have told me you were so young when we first met."

He chuckled. "I had no chance to say anything before you stabbed me."

"Sorry," I said.

"No. I deserved it. If I ever hurt you again, please stab me again."

I laughed.

"But I promise I'll do my best to never hurt you."

I nodded. "Ready to lose your virginity?"

He laughed. "I'm ready for anything with you."

Fallon released my hands, grabbed me around the waist, and hoisted me over his shoulder. His strength should have been surprising, but it wasn't after seeing him fight. After seeing him heft dead bodies around as though they didn't matter.

He strode toward the bed and tossed me onto the mattress. Fallon followed, kissing me with an urgency I sensed to my core. His hands stroked my bare skin in light teasing caresses making me squirm on the mattress. I rubbed myself against the hardness in his pants as I lifted my legs around his waist and lined us up perfectly. He rolled his hips into mine in a motion that occurred naturally between mates.

He didn't need to worry about this being his first time. Everything he was doing came so effortlessly that we could have been together a thousand times already.

"Clothes off," I said, shoving at his pants with my eager fingers.

He wrenched his clothes free barely stopping kissing me long enough to get each piece off before coming back and kissing me again. His lips trailed to the edge of my jaw. I ran my nails down his back sending shivers through his body.

Fallon sat back with a start.

"What's wrong? Did I hurt you?"

He shook his head and worried his lip between his teeth. "Can I..."

"What?"

"Can I tie your hands together?"

My eyebrows rose. "My hands?"

"Your touch is driving me wild. I want to touch you. Learn everything that makes you happy. When you're touching me all I can think about is your touch."

His words made me want to touch him even more. Drive him over the edge, but this was a partnership from here on out. I was no longer the one in control. We were in this together. I placed my hands together.

"I trust you."

"You do?"

"Aye. You were right. We should have marked each other as soon as possible. I understand you so much now after seeing your memories."

He untied the ribbon from my hair that he'd tied around his wrist and threaded them around mine sealing them together in a tight knot.

"Tell me if you want it off."

"I will. You realize I won't hold back."

He laughed. "I meant tell me with words instead of stabbing me with a dagger."

"They're all over there." I nodded at the wall.

"As if there isn't one under your pillow."

"Two actually." I grinned.

"Mate." He groaned. "So hot."

He kissed me then taking his time to learn every way I'd reposition my body against his depending on how he kissed me. Slow kisses made me rub my breasts against his chest. Hard kisses made me rub against his erection. His kisses traveled down my body to my breasts. He suckled the tight tips of my nipples into the warmth of his mouth. My back bowed from the bed, and I lowered my tied hands to his head urging him to keep going. He lifted my hands back over my head shaking his head at me.

Dia, I longed to touch him so much. Give him as much pleasure as he was giving me.

His mouth dropped back to my breast drawing the peak of my nipple into his mouth sending a pull of pleasure straight to my core. Every muscle drew tight in longing for him to bury himself deep inside me.

"I need you," I whispered.

"You have me."

"All of you. Now."

He rolled his hips against mine. The flared head of his cock brushed over the slickness between my legs.

"There." I arched my back.

He rolled his hips again. "Like this?"

"Aye. No."

He chuckled. "What do you want me to do?"

"Grab your cock and feed it into me bit by bit. I want to experience every inch of you entering me for the first time."

"Fuck, Aislinn. That's such a turn-on hearing you talk like that."

A scheming grin stretched my lips. At least now I appreciated he liked dirty talk in bed. It was so hard for me to know what he'd like since this was his first time and the only memories I'd seen in his mind of sexual pleasure were when he'd been with me.

He stared between us, watching as he did what I said. The blunt tip of his cock nudged my entrance. I blew out a breath trying to relax my muscles and make it easier for him to slide in. His other hand reached down and rubbed the tip of my clit making all my muscles clench in need once more. My legs shook as he held himself at my entrance while stroking my clit in a rhythm that had me seeing stars around his head. Would I come before he'd even made it inside me? Thrashing my head side to side I begged him to enter me. My words were incoherent to my ears, coming from a place deep in my heart that needed this man. My mate.

Fallon eased the tip of his cock inside. Sparks shot off inside me. It was too much and not enough. My begging continued and it must have got through to Fallon because he thrust in further while keeping up the strokes on my clit until my brain short-circuited even more. My core clenched and unclenched with each inch he eased inside me until he had to remove his hand from his cock. The moment he seated himself fully and his balls hit my ass, I came with another incoherent sound coming from my mouth.

His head dropped to my forehead. "You feel so good."

Every muscle in his body was tight as he held himself above me watching the pleasure run over my face and body. Tears welled in my eyes. Marking him had felt right. But this here. This was my new home.

I tilted my face and kissed him. He kissed me back with a slow drugging kiss and then he experimented with moving his cock with a slow roll of his hips that had my body surging with a fresh flood of desire for this man. The gentle thrusting soon turned to deeper, harder thrusts. Harder kisses too until our breaths grew ragged. Our bodies tightened to the peak of pleasure. I think tears might have even fallen from my eyes.

It was beautiful and raw.

Everything I'd ever wanted was now here with me.

My back arched off the bed. I wrapped my legs around his waist urging him to keep hammering into me in the same uncontrollable way he'd fallen into. His cock swelled inside me rubbing every inch of my sensitive flesh making me sense him and only him. My hands fumbled for him as I came again shuddering and shaking on his cock. The orgasm was even better than the first. My touch sent him into the freefall of bliss with me and his orgasm pulsed deep inside me heightening and lengthening my own.

His fingers tugged the ribbon free, and I ran my hands down his back enjoying the ripples of pleasure running over him at my touch. I'd lie here forever like this with him. I kissed the side of his face.

"Safe to say your first time was successful," I said.

He rolled off me laughing. I followed him, hugging my body to his, not yet ready to give up the connection. I'd never be ready for this to end.

We needed to fix the spring.

Now I had a mate, I wanted forever with him.

# CHAPTER TWENTY-FOUR
# FALLON

IN BED, AISLINN TURNED into a ball of cuddliness that surprised me. She clung to me between each round of sex, but I wouldn't have it any other way. We'd spent who knows how long in bed, but both our stomachs rumbled for food, so we decreed it was time to get dressed and return to the shit show that was at present happening in our lives.

To think before she'd turned up again, life had been easy with my long-found troupe of village friends standing by my side through the good and the bad times. It annoyed me Hamish left me when I was at my happiest. He was my closest friend. The person I'd often talk everything through, but he'd held onto the resentment of the King closing the Veil while I'd come to realize why the King had taken such drastic measures.

I'd do anything for my mate.

Aislinn had proven the same.

We made our way into the immense bathroom connected to her bedroom. The suite of rooms she lived in made my caravan pale by comparison. Her bedchambers were large. Opulent. Fine fabrics adorned the bed. Even finer paintings hung from the walls in the bathroom the only place they resided. I inspected one.

"Roisin's paintings," Aislinn said, pride tinging her voice.

"She's very talented. She'd make a fortune on Earth selling those."

"Money doesn't interest us the way it does humans."

"I had to learn to care about money while living so long on Earth. It was hard to get used to in the beginning."

Aislinn filled the tub with water and then lit the pile of wood beneath the enormous tub sitting in the middle of the bathroom. On one side was a window and outside the sky was a crystal-clear blue with not a single cloud on the horizon. The flock of phoenix flew by the window.

"Do the phoenix fly around a lot?"

Aislinn sat in the now filled and warm tub and crooked her finger at me.

"No."

"Strange," I said placing a palm to the window. "I've only been here twice, and I've seen them both times."

Aislinn dunked her head under the water and then rose back up, the soft pink peaks of her nipples bobbed on the surface of the water. "They only come out this much around mating time when they put on a display."

I stood for long moments soaking in the sight of my mate. Her damp hair hung over the creamy expanse of her skin. Skin I'd kissed in every single place and yet I still wanted more. I'd never get enough of her.

"Are you going to watch me all day or are you going to wash too?"

The teasing lilt in her voice had me striding toward her and lowering myself to the opposite end of the tub. It was so enormous that we both fit in with our feet brushing the toes of the others.

"This place is so different."

"To Earth, aye."

I picked up the bar of soap and scrubbed my arms. The sweet aroma of wildflowers filled the room adding to the heavy steam hanging in the air. Aislinn examined me the same way I'd observed her a few minutes ago. Our gazes falling often to the etched swirls embedded in our skin over our hearts where the Fae mating mark sat. Now we'd marked each other we could track the other no matter where they went.

A loud band echoed on her door then a second later the bathroom door flung inward. I jumped to my feet ready to defend her. My powers swirled around my hands without conscious thought when it came to defending my mate.

"Aislinn," her mother snapped, standing in the doorway. "What are you doing?"

My power disappeared in an instant as I covered my cock with my hands and tried not to blush.

"Bathing with my mate," Aislinn said. "Sit back down, Fallon."

I sank back into the water, grateful her mother could no longer see my naked lower half. The Queen's eyes landed on my marked chest. Her eyebrows rose high on her forehead, but then they dropped as she smiled. The change in her expression from seeing the fated mate mark went from angry to happy in the space of a second.

"You mated!"

"Aye." Aislinn returned her smile.

"I'm so happy for you. Both of you." She hugged her arms around her waist since she couldn't embrace her daughter in the bath. "Your father will be so happy to hear the news too. I'll tell him as soon as possible." She sighed as though there was a great worry on her mind. "I wish you'd told us together instead of me finding out like this."

Aislinn ducked her chin. "Sorry, we got a bit carried away."

That wasn't the entire reason.

Her mother's smile vanished. "I wish you hadn't thrown your guards away then traveled back here with no one knowing where you were or if you were safe. Your father put things in place for a reason. You all comprehend this, yet you all still go against him. Can't you see how much you're hurting him?" She sniffed.

Aislinn climbed out of the bath, draped a robe over her body, and walked toward her mother.

"Mother," she whispered. "I didn't mean to." Her throat worked on a hard swallow.

The Queen's face softened from her tirade as she hugged Aislinn briefly.

"How is Father? Did he sleep properly after our last visit?"

The Queen's eyes glistened. "He's sleeping now."

Aislinn's gaze flashed to the window. "Now? It's daytime."

"He's been in and out of consciousness since you were here last. When he's awake, he's delirious. I can't make out anything he's saying."

"What?" I climbed out of the bath too and grabbed the nearest towel to wrap around myself. "Won't the spring heal whatever's wrong with him?"

The Queen's lips trembled. "The spring is what's wrong with him."

"No." Aislinn gasped and covered her mouth with both hands.

The Queen's shoulders deflated. "He's been feeding his powers into the spring, keeping us all alive and now it's killing him."

"Mother, no." Aislinn sobbed.

She lunged for her mother, tugging her into the warm embrace of her arms as her entire body convulsed in a dreaded shiver.

"What can we do?" I asked.

"There's only one thing we can do. Cure the spring," the Queen said.

"How? I'm sorry, but from Aislinn's memories, you've been looking for a cure for years and haven't found it. How do we find one now?"

"Earth must have the answers. It's the one place we haven't exhausted our searches."

"Humans don't believe in magic anymore," I said.

"They might not believe it, but it still exists. There will be someone who can help or something to tell us what can help, I'm sure of it." She paced away again. "If we can find the source of the spring on Earth, then we might learn more about the cause of our problems."

"The source of the spring is on Earth?" I asked.

"Magic connects the two worlds. We were once the guardians of Earth. They welcomed our magic there. Humans treated us like gods because we helped everyone and then evil took it all away." She flung her arms out to the sides.

"Evil will always come," I said. "We have to be ready for that."

"We've prepared all these years. Trained to be fighters instead of the peace-loving Fae we once were. Evil won't defeat us again."

I stared at Aislinn. Her training with daggers made even more sense after hearing her mother talk. The scars from that night ran deep, but they'd made the Fae stronger too.

"No, it won't," I said. "I don't want to get your hopes up, but I know a place where my powers feel at peace in the same way they do here. It could be the connection you're looking for."

Aislinn's gaze shot to mine as though she'd just comprehended what she'd seen in my memories.

"The fountain in your old village?"

"It was the only place that calmed my powers," I said. "Until I traveled here that is."

The Queen's blue eyes lit with hope. "Take an entire contingent of guards with you."

"That won't be necessary," I said. "It would draw a lot of unnecessary attention to us."

"We'll handle this Mother." Aislinn placed her arms around the Queen and hugged her.

The Queen squeezed her back and then said, "For Dia's sake, at least take your guards with you."

"Yes, Mother," Aislinn said.

I smiled, for as much of a front as Aislinn put on for being the brutal, uncaring, killer, she had a warm, soft heart and an abundance of love for her family. I'd do anything to make sure she didn't lose her parents the same way I'd lost mine.

# CHAPTER TWENTY-FIVE
## AISLINN

I SHOULD HAVE KNOWN I wouldn't get more than a moment of happiness with my mate. Everyone believed being a Fae royal was the greatest thing, but the sacrifices we made for everyone else always came at a cost to us. Take my father who'd put his life on the line to keep everyone else alive and immortal. What had he been thinking?

If he died, we'd experience our greatest loss. My eldest brother Rian would become King, but he was with his mate on Earth who was the Queen of the Jungle. Would she give that up to be with Rian? Or would they spend their lives separately ruling two kingdoms as they'd already attempted to do before realizing fated mates needed to be together? I needed to stop Father dying, so I didn't have to worry about my brother and his mate too.

Fallon had a seriousness I hadn't seen before etched on his face as we walked back to the field and the tower. The scribe shook his head at us and Brogan and Conlan scowled so hard that I was afraid they'd look that way forever. I'd made a mess of things, and I couldn't help thinking I was to blame even though logically it was only the last day that I'd messed up.

What would the other Fae say if they realized I'd killed humans to protect my mate? Would they shrug and not care? Or would it appall them I was as blood thirsty as the King turned after the Trapper's destruction?

It was a moot point when we might all be dead soon. Well, soon instead of never. When you were immortal, the prospect of becoming mortal was like a punch in the stomach you didn't see coming.

We crossed through the Veil once again, this time landing on the soil of Ireland. The place held so many wonderful memories of my mother's parents. Yet it held the worst memories of my life too.

Fallon pulled me into his arms and tipped my chin up. "This is where we met."

I gave him a small smile. "The beginning and maybe the end."

He firmed his lips. "We'll never end. We're forever."

"Forever," I whispered, nodding.

The strength of my feelings for Fallon was growing every day. Every second we were together love blossomed inside my chest. It was at the point now that I wanted to tell him. Did he love me too? He'd shown me in small ways that he thought the world of me, but was that enough?

And why was I concerned with that right now?

In the distance, a cove curled around the village. I'd transported us through the Veil near my grandparent's farm hoping it was still secluded enough no one would notice our sudden appearance. As luck would have it, that's exactly how it was. The old farmhouse no longer stood where it once had. In its place stood a white two-story farmhouse with a thatched roof. So much larger than the tiny cottage that had once stood there. A pang of longing hurtled me back toward the past.

Fallon stared at the farmhouse and the soft gray smoke billowing out of the chimney into the gloomy sky.

"Is that where your grandparent's house used to stand?"

I nodded, unable to speak through the emotion clogging my throat.

"The new owners built a bigger house."

I nodded again. Nothing had stayed the same except for the farmland around the building, but that too didn't have the same crops. Different vegetation blew in the wind. My powers flowed to my hands ready to do away with the wind, but I lowered my hands instead and let the icy chill of the breeze beat against my cheeks like the slashes of a whip.

"Let's head into the village. Hamish and the others will be around the countryside somewhere, we'll find them after we visit the fountain."

A fountain that might be the source of our spring. I wanted to hope, but I had little inside me that a small fountain would be a place for all our magic. We traipsed down the hillside, Brogan taking the lead and Conlan in the rear.

I cleared my throat. "Sorry, I threw you across England."

Brogan gawked over his shoulder, but he said nothing.

"We were trying to protect you, Princess," Conlan said from behind.

I peered at Conlan over my shoulder. "I appreciate that, I do, and I understand I overreacted to those men taking Fallon, but when it comes to your mate..."

"We wouldn't know," Conlan said.

No, he wouldn't. There'd be so few matings in the Summer Court since the King closed the Veil. Even fewer births. Those that fell pregnant didn't always make it to term. Another thing Fallon and I hadn't discussed yet, but we'd have to before my next heat occurred, whenever that might be.

As we drew closer to the buildings, it became apparent the village was alive with people. They flung curious glances our way forcing Fallon to stop and enter a shop. He walked back out with a hat and slid it onto my head.

"That'll have to do. The rest of my money is with Hamish otherwise I'd buy you all new clothes." He slid his gaze over our attire.

More than ever, I sensed I stood out from the crowd. The humans were dressed in pants, long-sleeved tops, and thick jackets. While I was walking around in a dress in the cold weather, I was bound to get strange looks. The guards weren't too undressed, but their clothes looked out of place amongst the humans. We hurried along the cobblestone streets through the village. Colored houses lined the streets two stories high like the house standing in my grandparent's stead. At another time, I might have taken the time to admire the beauty of the place, but fear and worry were a constant companion inside me.

Fallon followed the streets taking us toward the end of the village near a great forest beyond. At the end of one street stood a high brick wall. A wooden door covered by vibrant green vines attempted to hide the door from view, but Fallon found it with the ease of someone who remembered where to look. He opened the door. Not a single sound emanated from it and considering the wood appeared as old as me that was saying something. Beyond the door was an overgrown garden. Roses bloomed everywhere. Vines clung to the thorny bushes as though trying to sample the sweet, perfumed blooms. We battled our way through the dense growth of once what would have been a garden to rival the one in the Summer Court.

At the furthest corner, we found another wall keeping all the wild vegetation inside. Briana would have a great time in here commanding these plants back under control with her powers, but she wasn't here. I was. Bright green moss covered the gray stones from the ground up to the trickle of water pouring from a small spout in the wall onto a platform that then fell onto the ground and disappeared beneath the stones underneath. Above the wall, the tree branches swayed, overshadowing the fountain as though trying to hide it from the world.

We stepped closer to the fountain.

"What are we doing here?" Brogan asked.

"Shh." I silenced him with a slash of my hand.

I clasped Fallon's hand in mine and took the last few steps to the fountain. Water as clear as our spring poured from the wall. With a shaking hand, I placed my fingertips into the slow but steady stream. Magic hit my fingers.

This was it.

This was the source of our Spring of Life right here on Earth. Right here in this small coastal village where anyone might access it. Why weren't guards around it? Why had we not known of its existence?

"Fallon," I said with wonder in my voice. "This is the place."

I eased closer to the water, desperate to touch more of it and make sure that what I was sensing wasn't a figment of my dreaming. My hand entered the stream of the water, turning it over, I cupped the water. It was magical. Soothing. I couldn't pull my hand away. It felt like our Spring of Life.

"Step away from the fountain," a gruff voice said. "No one is permitted to touch the water."

I turned from the fountain to the sight of Brogan and Conlan held at the end of swords aimed at their necks by men dressed in chainmail armor. Behind them stood at least twenty more men and women armed with swords.

A man with a long gray beard stepped forward. "We don't allow tourists here."

Fallon held up his hands and shuffled away from the fountain. I couldn't leave it though. This place might be where I fixed everything wrong back home.

"We're not tourists," Fallon said.

I wouldn't let anyone stand between me and this newfound hope for our future. Putting my hands behind my back where these humans wouldn't see the glow of my power, I summoned a wind strong enough to knock them off their feet. They landed in a heap grunting and groaning. I'd avoided my guards from the blast though and they now stood clear of the threat. Conlan collected the swords while Brogan dragged the old man to his feet and held the sword to his throat ready to slice it open.

"Who are you people?" Brogan ground out.

The old man's eyes landed on me. In particular, on my head where the hat had flown free in the breeze and my flower crown was now on display.

"A Fae princess," he said, awe tinging his voice.

All the fallen people on the ground scrambled to their knees and bowed.

What was going on? Who were these people?
And how did they know I was Fae princess?

# CHAPTER TWENTY-SIX
## AISLINN

**"F**ORGIVE ME, YOUR HIGHNESS." The older man bowed at the waist as his voice wobbled. "We would never stand in the way of Fae visiting the fountain."

"Who are you?" I placed my hands on my hips.

"I'm Alister O'Cuinn and we're The Fellowship of the Infinite Spring."

"What?" Fallon asked.

His confusion echoed mine but less eloquently. I'd never heard of these people.

"You are humans?" I asked.

"Yes." Alister placed a trembling hand over his heart. "We've pledged our lives to the service of the Fellowship. To the Fae."

"How have I never learned of you?"

"We're a secret society, Your Highness. We take great pride in keeping the secrets of the Fae."

"So secret that you keep them even from us?" I frowned.

"It's not our job to communicate with Fae."

"What is your job?" Fallon asked.

"Our job is to protect the fountain of eternal life. We allow no human in the presence of such magic for it corrupts them."

"We're not human, but you are. So why are you allowed here?"

"We're only allowed here after extensive training. Once the teachers are sure the magic of the water won't tempt us with its power, then and only then are we allowed into this sanctuary." He dipped his head. "Can the others stand now?"

"Aye." I clicked my fingers.

Brogan and Conlan stood on either side of me and Fallon, their tense bodies on alert against these humans who'd snuck up behind them and endeavored to incapacitate them. If they'd wanted, my guards could have broken free from their hold with their powers, but showing who and what we were to humans had held them back for the split moment it had taken for me to let my power control the situation.

The fellowship of twenty people stood their chainmail clinking with their movements as they reclaimed and sheathed their swords. Light glinted off the carved handles and for the first time since the man had spoken, I believed him. On the hilt of the swords were the same intricate swirls of knots that we embedded into the skin of our mates when we marked them. My hand touched my chest where Fallon had placed the same mark. There was no soreness associated with the mark, but there was a connection. Wherever my mate traveled, I'd track him. It sure would have come in handy when those men took him to the fighting ring.

"Can I ask a question?" Alister asked.

"You may." I inclined my head.

"Why are you here?"

I glanced back at the fountain. "We've been looking for the place where our two worlds are connected."

"Why? When you have the Spring of Life in the Summer Court."

I opened my mouth and then closed it again. Could we trust these people? These humans comprehended more about us than they should.

"You're wary. That's understandable after those filthy Trappers."

A murmur of agreement rumbled through the group.

"We lost many of our fellowship that night too protecting this place." He rubbed the gray hairs of his beard. "The stories passed down to us through the archives were hard to read."

"You have archives?"

"Yes. We have an extensive library."

"Where?" I asked searching the enclosed garden in hopes a magical library would appear before my eyes.

Perhaps this fellowship would have what we needed to find the cure to our spring? If we studied the magic of their fountain, could we use the magic in our spring?

"You're standing on it." He chuckled.

My gaze dipped to the ground. The only thing under my bare feet was the gray stones around the fountain. Where the people stood was thick vegetation.

Fallon crossed his arms. "Stop messing with us. All the times I've been to this fountain, and you never appeared. There was never a library here either."

"I'm serious. Follow us," Alister said.

The group turned and walked away from the fountain. I didn't want to leave because every ounce of my power recognized this place was important to the Fae, and these people comprehended things we didn't. How was it possible the Fae royals knew nothing about these people? About this fountain? And a library with information?

"Princess," Brogan said. "I'm not sure this is safe or wise."

"I agree," Fallon said. "We don't know these people."

"True, but I don't sense any malicious intent coming through the air from them." I fiddled with the hilt of one of my daggers under my dress. "I say we follow them."

Brogan and Conlan hadn't learned the dire straits of the spring. They didn't know about the King's deterioration either. Fallon met my gaze and nodded. He understood how urgent this was. If these people intended to hurt us, then we'd take them down. We'd never hesitate ever again.

Brogan huffed but followed the group of humans. Fallon fell into step behind him. I stuck close to my mate but not too close that I couldn't summon my powers. Conlan walked behind me muttering under his breath the entire time that he no longer wanted to be my guard. I almost laughed, but he had a point. We'd had nothing but trouble since coming to Earth.

Suddenly, the people disappeared one by one. As we got closer to the end of the line, stone steps leading below the ground came into view.

"I guess that's what they meant," Fallon said.

Every nerve in my body flared alive with powerful magic. So many welcoming vibrations emanated from the opening that I wanted to rush inside and soak in the atmosphere.

Brogan disappeared down the steps into the cavern underneath.

"Do you sense it?" I whispered to Fallon.

He shook his head and then followed Brogan down the stairs. I kept close to my mate, so close I was breathing on the back of his neck. The deeper we descended, the lighter it became as wall sconces flickered with an unnatural flame of iridescent white, so the place was brighter than anywhere I'd ever seen.

The group sat at a long wooden table running the length of the room which stretched for hundreds of feet.

Along the side walls were rows and rows of wooden shelves holding books of varying ages.

"Dia, Ciara would have a field day in here." I ran a finger over the closest volume.

"What is all this?" Fallon asked.

"The history of the Fae," Alister said.

"How do you have it, and we do not?" I asked.

Alister shrugged then undressed his chainmail. The other guards followed suit. So, he was their leader.

"Have a seat." He waved at the table and the space in front of him before sitting himself.

Fallon and I sat opposite him on the long bench seat. The person closest to us scooted along the seat giving us more space. Alister steepled his hands and placed his chin in them.

"I still can't believe I'm in the presence of a Fae princess. Feeling your power was incredible. I've read about it, but nothing can compare to experiencing it in the flesh." A slow grin formed on his weathered face. "I assumed I'd be like my father before me and never experience it."

A middle-aged woman leaned forward. "We're all honored you're here."

"But?" I asked.

"But why are you here?" she asked. "It's been centuries since we've seen or even heard of a Fae on Earth. We believed you'd forsaken our planet."

"Forsaken?" I frowned.

"You left us without your aid. The planet has suffered since your departure," she said.

"Fiona, enough," Alister snapped.

The woman blushed and sat back in her chair.

"Sorry about my daughter. She can be too outspoken," Alister said.

"We were unaware." I curled my fingers into my palms under the table forcing my power to stay quiet. An underground library full of precious books would be the last place for a whirlwind to form. "We have our problems too we've been trying to deal with."

"What problems?" Alister dropped his hands from his face and spread them on the table.

"I don't know if I can trust you."

"Fair." He nodded. "I don't know if I can trust you."

I puffed out a breath. We stared at each other in a stalemate. If I wanted this group of humans to help then I'd have to share what was wrong with the spring, but what if these people were like the others who wanted our powers?

What should I do?

Trust humans again and risk losing the only Fae that were left in existence?

Or not trust him and risk losing my father before I lost everyone else?

# CHAPTER TWENTY-SEVEN
## FALLON

"**T**HE OUTCOME IS WORTH the risk," I said, finding Aislinn's hand under the table and squeezing it. Her beautiful blue eyes with the indigo rims met mine and a wordless conversation passed between us. I told her without words that she had my support no matter what she did, but from her memories and what the Queen said about the King, we needed all the help available to us. We deserved our forever to be long. I wanted eternity with her. I didn't want a mortal lifetime. We'd already lost hundreds of years together. I wanted those years and more.

"Our Spring of Life is dying," Aislinn said.

A collective gasp resounded through the group and echoed through the room. Even Aislinn's guards gave an astonished grunt. Then silence descended, and all eyes landed on Alister.

"We suspected something was wrong," he said. "The fountain has been running slower each year. We believed the cause was one of the many problems with Earth, but if your spring is declining too, then... then... this is a greater problem."

I sighed. He didn't comprehend what was causing the problem. We'd trusted him with the knowledge for no reason. Tears formed in Aislinn's eyes. Her father would die soon. Sooner than any of us since he'd been feeding the spring his power. He'd weakened himself for us. Put his life before ours. I didn't want Aislinn to lose her father the way I'd lost mine.

She composed herself and said, "Is there anything in this library that would help?"

"Perhaps." He rubbed his beard again. "Everyone hit the books."

The entire group of people scrambled from their seats and started pulling books from the shelves. Soon they'd covered the entire table with open books.

I touched her elbow. "We need to meet up with my sister and Rory soon otherwise they'll be worried."

My sister and I had agreed to meet up at a specified time and place before traveling our separate ways here. If one of us didn't turn up on time, then we'd worry. I wouldn't do that to Erin. Not after the stress I experienced finding her all those years ago. We were in this together and that's why I had to stand by her choice to love a human.

"Is it far from here?" Aislinn asked.

"I'm not leaving you here," I said.

There was no way I'd let us become separated again.

"Of course not." She squeezed my thigh. "We stay together."

Nodding, I slid one of the open books in front of us. I'd studied over the many years, but it wasn't my favorite thing to do. My fingers flicked the pages, but I may as well have been looking at an unfamiliar language because nothing made sense to me.

"Does it make sense to you?" I whispered to Aislinn.

She bit her lip and nodded. "Ciara has made us all help her at some point or another, but she's the best person to ask about these books."

"We can transport her here."

"No. I still don't know if we should trust humans."

"We have to start somewhere."

Aislinn shook her head. "If something happened to her..."

"I get it, I do," I said running my fingers over her thick braid. "Family matters. I have a sister too."

"We should leave and meet up with Erin," Aislinn said.

The fellowship members stared at us when we stood as though they weren't sure if we were going to hurt them.

"We have to leave but we'll be back," I said.

Alister rushed over to us. "I'll walk you out."

I was sure we could find our way back up the stairs and out of the garden since I'd come to this place a few times over the many years, and I'd never seen these fellowship members. Why had they never come out when I'd been here? Was it because I'd never touched the water? Had Aislinn touching it triggered a warning system? Was the secret order so secret that the people they were protecting didn't even know about it? I suppose a secret society wasn't a secret if others knew about it, but one would think the two would work together. So why had they been kept separate? Or had the Fae lost the knowledge of these people over the years? Were there records inside the Summer Court that spoke of them? Aislinn hadn't mentioned them, and I'd seen no knowledge of them in her memories, so if there was a place in the Fae Kingdom that knew of them, then where was it? And who was it? Or did whoever know about the society assume they'd all died because they were human?

"It will annoy my grandson he wasn't here to meet you," Alister said while walking us up the stone stairs. "He's away on a training mission. We'll soon induct him into the fellowship."

The pride coming from Alister's voice was the same I used to hear in my father's voice. No matter the length of time, I missed him and my mother.

"How long has the fellowship existed?" I asked.

"For as long as there have been Fae and humans."

"That was a long well-kept secret," Aislinn said. "Why are you telling us now?"

"Your Spring is dying. So is Earth. If we don't fix what we've broken, then we'll all die." He patted me on the shoulder as we breached the top of the stairs before my tall frame towered over his. "You are our only hope."

And here I'd believed there was just the Summer Court's problems to deal with. I'd had my rage-filled head hidden for so long that I hadn't detected what the old man was telling us. The Earth had changed since the King closed the Veil, but everything had changed.

"I'm guessing you'll lose your powers with the spring's demise?" Alister asked.

Shit, I hadn't even considered that. To be powerless and mortal? I'd kept my powers a secret for so long, that when I was in the Summer Court, it was more natural to let that control go. More natural to use them than to keep them inside.

I rubbed a hand over Aislinn's mating mark on my chest. If we lost our powers, then I'd lose the ability to track her. If we were parted, then I wouldn't be able to find her. I never wanted to experience that ever again.

"Perhaps," was all I said.

He walked us through the thick, overgrown vegetation as though he was walking along a path. The door was easy to see from this side of the wall.

"We can't have that. We'll need your powers to fix Earth." He nodded to himself. "Come back as soon as you can, and I promise we'll find an answer to your problem."

How could he promise? That was one strong promise to make. Either the man knew the answer already or he understood where to look. I opened the door, the sooner we met with Erin and Rory, the sooner we'd come back here and find a cure. Brogan stepped through the door first, scanned the area outside then nodded for us to follow. We all walked through the door and back into the streets of Ireland.

A gray drizzle of rain fell on our heads, and I gawked back at the garden surprised to see the rain wasn't falling into the walled-in area. Aislinn followed my gaze.

"What sort of magic surrounds this place?

"I don't know," I said, taking her hand in mine. "I've always sensed peace in there near the fountain."

"I did too."

"Same," Brogan said.

Conlan nodded his head.

"So they don't mean us any harm?" Aislinn frowned.

"It might be hard to believe, but not all humans are evil."

"I recall a time they loved us," Aislinn said. "A time we lived in peace and harmony."

"I sometimes forget how old you are and seeing your memories, it was as though you lived in another time and place. I've been around long enough to see the changes here on Earth, but you missed all those."

Her eyes lit with understanding. "I witnessed them in your memories."

"Is the spring truly dying?" Brogan asked.

Aislinn nodded her head somberly. "Please keep it to yourselves."

Brogan and Conlan exchanged a worried glance but nodded their heads at Aislinn's request.

We left the quiet street with the magical garden and fountain and made our way along the busier streets once again receiving curious glances from the humans. We needed to change clothes, so we'd blend in, but to do that I'd have to find Hamish, so I'd get my money. Once we met up with Erin and Rory, then we'd find the others.

We walked fast through the village and followed the faint trail into the wooded forest. The deeper we traveled, the less the path was obvious. Memories assaulted me of all the times I'd played here as a child. When I'd swung branches with Hamish in pretend sword fights. Hide and seek with Erin when she was old enough. The many days I'd climbed the old, twisted wood of my favorite tree only to slip on the moss and fall to the ground. No matter how many times I'd struggled to make it to the top, I'd never succeeded.

"I recognize this place from your memories," Aislinn said.

"I spent a lot of time here."

"You did." She smiled. "I think I only ever explored here once when I was younger. I preferred spending time on the farm with my grandparents. This is where Erin and the others hid, wasn't it?"

"Yes. Erin was used to playing hide and seek in here so when the Trappers attacked it came naturally to her to hide in the forest."

"I'm so glad they never found her." She placed her palm on my shoulder and rubbed the tension forming in my back.

"Me too," I said.

"Boo," Erin called from the tree above us.

Aislinn's guards snapped their powers to their hands so fast that no one else had time to react. A bolt of power struck the tree knocking Erin and Rory to the ground. Erin squeaked as she hit the soil. Rory landed with a solid thump and didn't utter another word.

"Rory?" Erin yelled, scrambling across the dirt to his side.

He lay at an awkward angle. His arm bent behind his back in a way that shouldn't be possible. Rory's eyes were closed.

"Shit." I raced to his side and searched for a pulse.

A tiny flicker pumped under his skin.

"He's alive," I said, sinking onto my knees.

"Rory?" Erin sobbed.

"Sorry," Brogan said. "After everything that's happened today, I was on edge. My powers —" He waved his hands in the air.

He was having a hard time controlling his powers like I had the entire time on Earth even after visiting the fountain. That didn't bode well for our future.

"We need to find the others. Hamish and his sister Leah can fix him."

Leah had studied more medicine than anyone else over the years and learned everything there was about human medicine. Her and Erin were close, so they always made friends with humans together. Rory groaned and then his eyes flickered open.

"What happened?" he rasped.

"You fell from the tree," I said.

"They knocked him from the tree," Erin ground out through clenched teeth and shot a murderous look at Aislinn's guards.

"I said I was sorry," Brogan said. "I don't know what's wrong with me." He shook his head and his hands. "I usually have more control over my powers."

"It's being here on Earth and not being able to connect with the Summer Court. It makes our powers more volatile. We've struggled with it for years. The fountain helped for a time after we visited it."

"Shite," Brogan said. "We should get you all to the Summer Court."

"Aye," Aislinn said. "We need to convince them to leave if only for a short time."

"I'll carry him." Brogan scooped Rory off the ground making him cry out in agony.

Rory's arm hung limply by his side.

"This way," I said. "The others will have set up camp in the usual place."

# CHAPTER TWENTY-EIGHT
## AISLINN

T HE BRIGHT CARAVANS SAT in a small clearing beside the woods. The curved roofs were an array of colors in the gloomy sky. Each caravan had wooden doors with carved designs on them. Some were even etched with gold paint. They were so pretty. Scattered across the ground were bright red, blue, and yellow throw cushions on matching blankets. It was so similar to the place in England, I might have blinked and imagined we were in the same place. The group sat beside a small campfire on the blankets singing songs of all things. The second they noticed us, the charming singing stopped. They were so good, they might rival my mother for their talented voices except Mother's voice had the gift of power inside it.

After seeing Fallon's memories, I understood this tight-knit group a lot more. They were a family, and I'd come in and torn it apart. That wasn't what I wanted. Family was important to me. It was important to all Fae. It's why fated mates were so sought after. Surely, they weren't so upset with Fallon for finding me, that they'd up and leave without him?

Hamish strode forward, a deep scowl on his face. "What happened to Rory?"

Brogan lowered Rory to his feet but kept a steadying hand on his back.

"An accident with a tree and Aislinn's guard. I fell on my arm and broke it," Rory said.

"I can see that." Hamish scowled even harder. "Why didn't you take him to a hospital?"

"You and your sister know how to set broken bones," Fallon said.

"He's human."

"So?" Fallon asked. "Since when has that stopped you from helping?"

Hamish glanced away at the ground as though the dirt beneath our feet was important.

"What has gotten into you lately?" Fallon asked. "We've been friends for so long. Is it my fated mate who's bothering you?"

Hamish's gaze skidded my way. My muscles tensed in preparation to defend myself, or to convince his friend to give us a chance.

"You left us for the royals. For the ones who locked us out!"

Fallon opened his mouth, but Hamish continued his tirade.

"You left us. Went to the Summer Court when you knew none of us wanted to go. We didn't want you to go either."

"Hamish." Fallon ground his teeth.

"No. As soon as she appeared you forgot about us. We're your family. We've stuck together and now you're breaking us apart."

Hamish swung at Fallon. His fist connected with Fallon's face. A dull thud echoed through the shocked quiet of the bystanders. Hamish hit him again.

"Stop," I cried.

"This is all your fault," Hamish yelled at me and swung again.

Fallon let him hit him, obviously not wanting to hurt his friend, but I wouldn't stand by and let Hamish hurt my mate. Especially now when the spring was almost at an end. When our wounds might not heal. Power flared to my hands.

"No," Fallon said, snapping out of his passive stance.

I hesitated. Hamish swung again. Fallon's lip split open. Bright red blood marred his mouth.

"Enough!"

Using my power, I lifted Hamish into the air. He wriggled and thrashed his arms and legs but no matter what he did, he wouldn't break the hold my power had over him.

"Let me down. If it wasn't for you, none of this would be happening."

"She didn't fate us to be together you fool," Fallon said.

Was the declining spring affecting everyone and not just the royal family? I threw Fallon an appreciative glance. His bloody lip was already swelling. I gasped and rushed to his side.

"Your face."

"I'll be all right."

"No." I shook my head. "You don't understand. Your last bruises I had to heal with the spring's water. They weren't healing by themselves."

"Shit," Fallon said. "This is worse than I thought."

"It is." I grimaced.

"What are you two talking about?" Hamish asked from high above our heads.

Fallon and I exchanged a glance. Should we tell them?

"Have you calmed down now?" Fallon asked.

"No," Hamish seethed.

"You're just as bad as the King wanting to keep us separate still."

"Don't you say that," Hamish growled.

"It's the truth. But at least the King didn't know we existed. You're worse."

"I am not." Hamish thrashed his arms and legs again trying to get down or get to Fallon.

He'd never lay another fist on him.

"What are we going to do?" I asked.

I couldn't let Hamish down otherwise he'd hurt Fallon again.

"You can both leave. We don't want you here."

Fallon's face fell. After all he'd done to save them, to keep them together, and treat them all like his family and this was the thanks he got from them. From his friend. I lowered Hamish to the ground but kept a vortex of air surrounding him so he couldn't come near us.

"We'll leave," I said. "I hope you come to your senses and see the opportunity there is for others to find their fated mates in the Summer Court."

Hamish scowled. "Take Rory into my caravan. I'll set his arm, but he can't stay here."

"Don't worry, I don't want to stay where I'm not welcome," Rory said.

Erin sniffed back tears. Hamish's gaze landed on her face, then softened.

"Oh," I said. "You're in love with Erin."

"What?" Fallon, Hamish, and Rory all said at the same time.

"It makes sense now why you left without her as well as us."

"I am not." Hamish puffed out his cheeks as they reddened.

"My sister?" Fallon swung at Hamish so fast that no one saw it coming. Hamish's head flung back as Fallon's fist connected with his jaw. A loud crack rent the air sounding like bones might have been shattered. Hamish placed a hand over his jaw.

"Stop," Erin cried rushing between them.

Hamish swung at Fallon, but Erin was between them. His fist hit her in the chest and sent her flying across the ground. She groaned.

"What did you do?" Rory rushed Hamish not caring he already had a broken arm.

Hamish's hands flared a vibrant red, power flared in a red-hot flash. The dagger at my hip ripped from the holster with a surge of power that wasn't mine and hurtled through the air, landing in Rory's chest with deadly accuracy. Rory's feet stumbled on the ground. Erin gasped. The entire moment happened so fast. Rory's body slumped onto Hamish's chest, but he stepped back, so he fell to the ground with a thump that sounded final.

"Rory." Erin gulped.

"What did you do?" Fallon dropped to the ground and flipped Rory over.

Seeing my dagger protruding from his chest made my legs shake. How was this possible? How had my dagger killed him when I didn't throw it?

"I didn't do it," I whispered, the horror of the moment settling like a lump of stone inside my stomach.

Fallon felt for a pulse and shook his head. Erin wailed. Her face paled to ashen snow. She wobbled on her legs much like I was, but instead of staying upright, she collapsed onto the ground. Her sobs shook her body. Fallon rushed to her side and wrapped his arms around her rocking her limp body back and forth. I placed my hands over my aching heart. The anguish she must be experiencing... I thought I'd been in heartache when

Fallon left me the day we met, but now that I loved him I couldn't imagine the agony of losing him.

Fallon glared at Hamish.

Hamish folded his arms and glared back.

"Why did you do it?" he asked again.

"My power reacted to the threat."

"He was human. He had no weapons on him. And he had a broken arm. What threat would he be to you?"

Hamish shrugged. "We can't trust humans."

"You. We can't trust you," Fallon said. "You used your powers and stole Aislinn's dagger to hurt an innocent man."

"What?" I asked shock rolling through the lump in my stomach.

"Hamish has power over metals. He can command them to his will."

"He's the one who stabbed Rory? Not me?"

Fallon frowned. "You did nothing wrong, Aislinn."

"But if I didn't have daggers on my body, then he wouldn't have used them."

"Hamish would have used a knife by the fire."

"But it was my knife." I sucked in a shaking breath. "I'm so sorry Erin. If it wasn't for me, then Rory wouldn't be dead."

Erin buried her face into Fallon's chest. This was it. This was the moment I'd feared. Fallon would choose his sister over me. She was the one hurting. She was the one who needed his love and support the most right now.

"Aislinn stop blaming yourself." Fallon tried urging Erin away, but she clung harder to him.

"I'll leave. The problems with your family are all because of me."

"They're not." Fallon shook his head.

"Go," Hamish ground out dropping his hand away and revealing his jaw was still in one piece although a nasty red mark now lined it. He might be lucky and only have a bruise that might not heal.

"Erin shouldn't have been with a human." Hamish stomped his foot. "Fae should wait for their fated mate."

"Fallon and I waited, and we were miserable for hundreds of years. If you love Erin, and I say that as you are a member of her family, you all are." I waved my hand around the group. "Then wouldn't you have wanted her to be happy? You didn't need to kill Rory."

Hamish opened his mouth and then snapped it shut before any words flew out.

"Fallon marked me. I've seen his memories of you, and how much he loves you all. You're his family along with his sister. I'd like to get acquainted with his family better. I'd like you to get to know me. No one is trying to take anyone away from anyone. We're not trying to force you into the Summer Court."

"Fallon is our leader in my eyes and the eyes of everyone here. We don't want to go to the Summer Court and meet the Fae King. We don't want to be under his rule."

Sensing I wouldn't get anywhere with Hamish, I said, "All right. I'll leave."

"Aislinn, wait for me."

"You're needed here right now, Fallon." I gave him a sad smile. "You'll always be their leader. You're the head of your family and that's different to the King. They can have you lead your family. As for the ruling, you'll find the King…" I wet my dry lips.

Fallon reached a hand for me, but I couldn't get between him and his grieving sister. As much as I wanted to feel the comfort of his palm against mine.

"The King is a fair ruler. All he wants is to keep us safe. He's sorry he locked us out and if he'd known about us, he would have come for us," Fallon said.

"But he didn't come. He sent his daughter," Hamish said, keeping the fuel of hatred going.

"He had to send Aislinn. It was destined to be. What if your destinies, your fated mates, are in the Summer Court waiting for you right now?"

A ripple of murmurs ran through the troupe.

It tore my heart apart wishing I could help her, but Erin was bound to blame me for Rory's death. Even if I knew I didn't kill him. Even if everyone knew I didn't kill him, guilt still churned in my stomach that if I wasn't here right now Rory would still be alive.

I couldn't stay and wait for Erin to stop grieving long enough to forgive my hand in her loved one's death knowing my father was bedridden and delirious. How would the Fae cope without their king? I blinked back the tears gathering in my eyes as I couldn't let myself think he wouldn't be okay. Without my father in my life,

I'd break into a thousand pieces. He was our greatest support.

Being mortal would be the worst thing ever. Everyone I loved would die the way Rory had just died. I wouldn't let that happen.

Fallon's concerned eyes met mine over the top of Erin's head. He must have seen the fear on my face that I couldn't stop the spring from dying because he whispered in Erin's ear and eased her away so he could stand and walk toward me.

"I'll come with you," Fallon said.

"Come when you can." I cupped his face between my palms.

"Well, about time," Hamish said, placing his hands on his hips.

"You know where to find me when you sort this out." I touched my lips against his fighting back the tears in my eyes.

"I'll talk to them, then I'll come for you."

# CHAPTER TWENTY-NINE
## FALLON

WATCHING AISLINN TURN HER back and walk a few steps away was harder than living centuries on Earth alone without her. Now I'd had her love, there wasn't a moment I could live without it. I couldn't let her leave like this.

"Is he really gone?" Erin asked.

Her bottom lip wobbled. Tear tracks stained her cheeks. Her eyes were hollow like all the light and love had left them.

"I'm so sorry, Erin. He is. Hamish killed him."

Erin's waterlogged eyes snapped to Hamish. She scrambled to her feet.

"You!"

Hamish folded his arms. "I did you a favor."

How was this the same man I'd lived with for centuries? The same man who'd been my friend. I didn't recognize him. Was the spring so depleted that it had changed him this much, or had he always had an evil streak to him that I'd failed to see?

"A favor?" She stepped closer to him and poked him in the chest. "You hit me too. I thought we were family. Who hurts their family?"

"She's right," I said. "I'm so upset with you."

"What did I do?" Hamish threw his arms up in the air, his power flaring to his hands.

Erin gasped, and so did everyone else as all the knives lying beside the campfire kitchen floated in the air.

"Hamish you need to calm down."

"Calm?" he sneered. "It's all your mate's fault."

The knives spun in the air. I couldn't let him hurt anyone else. Let alone Aislinn. His anger toward my mate was misplaced. Her back was to us and those of her guards as she inched further away from the campsite giving me the chance to heal things with my troupe. But everyone thought they were immortal and invincible and what if Hamish throwing the blades killed them too because of the problem with the spring? And Aislinn. What if he hurt her and she didn't survive?

My power flared with the protective urge over my mate and slammed a bolt of lightning into Hamish. He screamed. His body flared on fire. His sister screamed and ran toward him, but others caught her in their arms, holding her back. I stared in horror at my best friend, burning alive. I didn't want to hurt him. All I'd wanted was to protect my mate and everyone else.

Aislinn rushed back into the campsite. Her palms glowed a radiant purple, then a breeze flew around Hamish, circling and smothering the flames until they were no longer burning. Hamish fell to the ground, sobbing in agony. His flesh was red and blistered the same way Aislinn's feet were the night we met. The memories made me shake. How had I caused this?

"I'm sorry, Hamish," I said, squeezing the words out of my dry throat. Were my powers unpredictable now too?

Aislinn wrapped her arms around my neck and drew my head to the crook of her neck. I let her hold me. Took comfort in the embrace of my mate. Her mere presence settled my powers. Hamish had acted atrociously, but he didn't deserve to be burned alive. No one deserved that. I hadn't meant to set him on fire.

"Will he die?" I asked, releasing Aislinn and staring at his burned body.

"Not if he has direct contact with the spring," Aislinn said. "Conlan, can you take Hamish to the Summer Court?"

Conlan scowled. "Might be better if he was dead."

"No." Aislinn shook her head. "He might be in the wrong, but it's not our decision to end his life. He needs to face the King."

"Great," I said. "Another reason for Hamish to hate the King."

Aislinn sighed. "It's up to you Fallon as his leader. Do you want him healed and held accountable for his actions, or do you want to do nothing and let him suffer?"

She didn't say die, because she didn't want the others to panic and know our wounds weren't healing properly. As much as Hamish had hurt us all today, I didn't want my friend to die.

"Do it." I nodded.

"Heal him and put him in the dungeon," Aislinn said.

Conlan stepped forward, slung Hamish over his shoulder, and parted the Veil. A moment later they disappeared into the swirling mist.

"We need to return too," Aislin said. "But first we have to check in with…"

"I know." I slung an arm around her waist. "Thank you for coming back for me."

She smiled. "I didn't want to leave, but I thought it would be easier for everyone here if I did."

"Don't do it again. Easy or not, we see everything through together."

"Aye." She bit her bottom lip making me want to suck it into my mouth, but now wasn't the time.

Everyone was sad and quiet. The events of today had shaken them all. No one wanted to stay, and I didn't blame them. Hamish's actions had tarred the image of our once peaceful lifestyle. Erin sat on the steps of her caravan staring into space. I didn't know how to make this better for her, so I hugged her again, told her to pack her favorite things and we'd be back soon to take her to the Summer Court.

Hopefully being in the Fae Kingdom would bring her the same sense of peace it brought to me, but I feared today would always mar her life. I could only hope she'd meet her fated mate, and he'd be the one to fix her broken heart.

Promising we'd return soon, we hurried back to the village, determination spurring me to lengthen my stride. The fear for the spring and her father's life, for all our lives etched across Aislinn's face did strange things to me. I didn't want to see it there. The first night we met fear had filled us both. I'd make sure we fixed what was wrong.

Not that I comprehended how, but I was willing to try everything.

Anything.

I needed her to be happy.

Right now, she was content she'd found me and marked me, but that fear for our future sat heavy in both our hearts. I wished I could take her in my arms and whisper everything would be okay, but I wouldn't lie to her. How could I guarantee it when I hadn't even considered Hamish would do the things he did?

At this late hour of the night, the village was dark and deserted. The windows in the homes were even darker. A breeze blew through the town carrying salt water on the wind. Aislinn's thick braid didn't shift an inch though. Her guards were as always protecting her, but I'd protect her even more than they would.

Before I unlocked the door to the garden, a man holding a lantern in his hand opened it.

"We've been waiting for you," he said.

"Have you found what we need?"

"I'll let the boss tell you that," he said with a grunt as he led us into the thick, overgrown garden.

"Why don't you keep the garden nice?" I asked.

"Keeps most tourists out," he said. "No one likes a raggedy garden, but they all flock to a pretty one."

"I suppose."

"We used to keep it nice. Before my time, that was. Then when that evil man found the place and destroyed the world as we knew it, we changed. I suppose everyone did."

"Do you mean the Trappers?" Aislinn asked.

"Yeah." He ground his jaw.

"It started here?" I asked.

He nodded. "It's why we protect it better now. This wall wasn't here before then."

"Why don't we know any of this?" Aislinn asked, her voice tinged with hurt.

I understood why she'd be upset. The Fae royals were the protectors of the spring in the Summer Court, but here on Earth, they weren't. A fellowship of humans were the protectors on Earth, and they'd failed at their job and almost caused all the Fae to die. I wanted to hate them, but the anger didn't come. The past was past. The future was the only way forward.

And forward was what we needed to concentrate on right now.

Behind us, Conlan cursed as his clothes caught on a branch and the sound of it echoed through the quiet garden. Another time and place, and I would have laughed.

The man disappeared down the stone stairs. The golden glow of his lantern led us into the depths of the underground library. We followed him down the steps. A buzz of conversations rippled through the fellowship.

Alister rushed forward, catching Aislinn's hands then thinking better of it and dropping his hands by his side.

"I'm so glad you returned. I half thought I'd imagined that a Fae princess had visited us." He laughed. "But then I reminded myself that we'd trained for this moment our entire lives."

"Trained for meeting me?" Aislinn asked, an amused smile on her face.

"Yes. No." He shook his head. "For helping the Fae to restore what once was."

Aislinn shook her head. "That sounds impossible."

"Improbable." He shrugged. "But meeting a Fae princess was that too. Yet here we are."

Fiona stepped forward. "We found what you need."

"You did?" Aislinn asked, the hope in her voice about felled me.

"Once the King opens the Veil, it will cure the Spring of Life." He grinned triumphantly.

With the King delirious and out of action, opening the Veil in its entirety would be impossible.

"The King has opened the Veil. How else are we here?" Aislinn asked.

Even if it was only a doorway, the Veil was open and if what Alister said was true, then the spring should have picked up, not declined.

He frowned. "But?"

Alister frowned and lifted a heavy tome from the table "This book has everything you need on the Spring of Life. There are other books, but this one should do it."

"Should?" I asked.

"You're welcome to read through the other books." He pointed at the many shelves lined with rows and rows of books.

It would take a long time to read them all, let alone the thick volume he held in his hands. Time that we didn't have.

"Can I take this one to the Summer Court with me, please?" Aislinn asked. "My sister Ciara is the bookworm. She'd understand it better than me."

"No, no. All the books must stay here."

Aislinn sighed.

"She can come here," Alister said.

"She's never left the Summer Court," Aislinn admitted.

Alister shrugged. "The books stay here in this library."

Aislinn paced away, threw her glowing hands up in the air, then lowered them back down before a gust of wind burst free from them.

"Can you tell us what's inside the book?" I asked.

"There are a lot of things in the book." Fiona took the book from her father, laid it on the table, and flipped it open. She scrolled through many pages and slapped a finger on the page. "This part talks about water magic." Her lips pursed. "Could that cause your spring's problems? Can magic stop it?"

"Water magic?" Aislinn asked. "I'm not sure. What else does it say?"

"Sorry, I haven't read it all yet. It's written in Old Norse and I'm slow at translating it," Fiona said. "I'll keep translating and reading and the others will keep looking in other books."

I slid my palm under Aislinn's hand on the dagger and wrapped my fingers around hers.

"Let's head to the Summer Court and talk to Ciara."

She nodded her head and squeezed my hand thanking me without a sound for always being there for her.

"We'll keep an eye out for your return," Alister said. "And we'll keep researching."

It was the best we could hope for in this moment. Time was not on our side, but whatever time we had left, I'd spend it with my mate.

# CHAPTER THIRTY

# AISLINN

RETURNING TO THE SUMMER Court with Fallon's troupe was exciting, but the fear I kept hidden churned my stomach into knots. The scribe was ecstatic and spent a long time talking with them, learning their history, and writing it down. Erin was quiet and sullen, I wasn't sure if she'd ever talk to me again, but I'd try my best to help her over her broken heart. She was now part of my family and we always stuck by each other through the good and the bad. It's what we did. She declined to come to the palace with us and instead stayed with the troupe. I didn't blame her actions as they were the people she was most comfortable with. The ones who had loved her for years. Their support during her darkest moment was what she needed. She also needed her brother, so Fallon promised he'd check in on her soon. We both would.

We left everyone with the scribes and the guards because we didn't want to waste any more time. They'd find a place for them to stay together. They needed each other right now, but we needed them too. Together we'd heal.

Fallon and I lost our guarded escort inside the Summer Court. It was a relief to no longer worry about Brogan and Conlan learning about the spring's problems. They knew, but they'd promised to keep the secret. The longer we kept it hidden, the less likely everyone was to panic.

I was panicking enough for everyone.

Grier opened the palace door, a grim look on his face. He'd seen a lot over his many years, but these last few years had weathered him. The last few days had worn me out. I longed to curl up in my bed and sleep. When was the last time I'd slept?

"The King and Queen are in their bed chambers. As are everyone else."

"Everyone?" I asked.

"Aye." He nodded.

That didn't sound good. I rushed through the marble hallways of the palace with Fallon right beside me holding my hand. He gave me the strength to shove open the door. It slammed shut behind us and my entire family lifted their heads at our abrupt arrival.

Father lay on the bed not moving.

"No," I cried, walking toward him on shaky legs that didn't feel like they'd keep me upright, but Fallon's firm arm around my waist kept me moving forward.

"Pepper made him a sleeping potion," Lorcan said, his arms draped over the shoulders of his mate. "It was the only way we were able to get him to sleep."

"He was delirious," Briana said. "Rambling about nonsense."

She stepped back into her mate, Sledge, who rubbed her back.

Mother wiped her eyes. I rushed over and hugged her. She squeezed her slender arms around me comforting me when I was trying to comfort her.

I pulled back. "We found something in Ireland."

"Ireland?" Mother shifted away. "What were you doing there?"

"We followed Fallon's troupe there to convince them to come to the Summer Court."

Mother sat on the side of the bed next to Father, her face as pale as the sheets draped over the King.

"My powers took us out of the Veil near our grandparent's farm. The cottage is no longer there."

A tear dripped onto Mother's cheek, and she wiped it away before more fell.

"It's strange seeing how much Earth has changed from what we knew it to be." I rubbed a hand over my aching chest.

Saoirse handed her baby to Arrow and hugged me.

"I understand what you mean. The more time I spend there, the more I realize how much it needs us."

I nodded my head. "I think we need each other. The humans and the Fae."

"What are you saying?" Ciara asked.

She and Roisin didn't have mates, but they stood beside each other in sisterly support.

"We found the place where the spring connects the two worlds."

Gasps rippled through the room.

"Did you fix it?" Rian asked, then shook his head. "No, we would have sensed it."

"We also found a group of humans protecting the corresponding fountain of magical water."

"They haven't performed a very good job," Rian mumbled.

"Agreed," Lorcan said.

"Shh," Ciara said. "Let Aislinn talk."

Nodding my thanks at Ciara, I told them everything we'd found, and everything we'd learned.

"If opening the Veil will fix the spring, then can't we do it?" Roisin asked.

I shook my head. "No, only Father's powers will open the Veil."

"But you all were unlocking it with your powers before, why can't you unlock the entire Veil?" she asked.

Mother sighed. "It's not that easy, Roisin. The King's powers are greater than you realize. You children might manipulate them to some extent, but you'll never override them entirely."

"Shit," Sledge said. "If the King is the only one who can fix it, then we need him awake."

"Waking him won't do anything," Pepper said. "Rian said he's diminished his powers with how he's been feeding it into the spring, besides, he's too out of it to comprehend what he has to do."

"They also said water magic might be able to affect the spring," Fallon said.

"Right. I forgot that part."

"Water magic?" Saoirse asked. "Like mine? Are you saying another Fae is hampering the spring?"

I shrugged. "The fellowship couldn't say, and they wouldn't let us take any books with us. We'll head back and research."

"I'll go too," Ciara said. "I'm the best at researching books."

"You've been researching for too long and have found nothing."

She placed her hands on her hips. "I'll have you know, I found something about that strange place above the waterfall."

In the town where the wolf shifters resided, Saoirse told us of a waterfall she felt a connection with which she'd hoped was the place connecting our two worlds. But it wasn't. Upon closer inspection, Briana discovered the area around the waterfall was surrounded by powerful magic. She'd helped Saoirse give birth there. They'd spoken of the beauty and magic of the moment. And when Rian and Sophia investigated the area further, they found a secret tunnel high above the waterfall, but they'd exited the tunnel into a place filled with booby traps which had forced them to leave without learning the secrets of the place. We all still believed there was something there to help us. Otherwise, why would we be drawn to the place? Why would it be so well protected? There were secrets there we'd yet to unravel.

"You did?" Sledge asked. "Let's hear it then."

Ciara blushed. "It was more of a reference to um... ah..."

"Spit it out," Sledge said.

"Orgies." Ciara's blush deepened.

I couldn't stop the laugh building in my chest from coming out of my mouth. I laughed hysterically, wiping tears from my eyes. Everyone laughed too and Ciara's face reddened so much, she stomped toward the door.

"Wait," I called. "What do orgies have to do with the spring?"

"I'm not sure yet, but I'll find out. I'm packing a bag, then we'll go to Earth to this secret library, and I'll find what we need." Tears welled in her eyes. "I have to."

All laughter stopped. We all understood the emotions inside her.

"I believe in you," Roisin said.

Ciara smiled at her and then left the room.

"I'm sorry I don't have more answers," I said.

"You've given us a lot," Rian said. "You look tired. When was the last time you rested?"

I rubbed my forehead. "When we were in the Quiet."

"You mated?" Saoirse shrieked loud enough to startle Ailbhe into crying.

"Yes," Fallon said.

"We want to hear details," Briana said. "But I agree with Rian, you look terrible."

"I feel terrible."

Fallon rubbed the tense muscles between my shoulders.

"Go rest while Ciara packs. She's no doubt filling a case with her most beloved books and deliberating over which ones to take. You have a bit of time," Briana said.

What she said was true, but how would I rest when everything hinged on finding whoever was using water magic on the spring?

Lorcan stepped forward, holding his palm out with a small potion bottle. "Pepper said this will rejuvenate you if you have a short sleep."

A potion from a witch? I shouldn't trust her, but my brother loved her, trusted her. The past was the past. I collected the bottle from Lorcan's outstretched hand and stared at Pepper.

"Thank you."

"A drop for both of you is all it takes, and you'll have sweet dreams."

I didn't know about sweet dreams, but sleep sounded good to me. Fallon looked as tired as I felt. My mate needed rest too. We left the King's and Queen's bed chambers. Lorcan followed me out the door and clasped my shoulder, halting me.

"Is he the reason?" he asked.

"What reason?" I tilted my head to the side.

"The reason you were in a bad mood for centuries." His gaze flickered to Fallon standing a short distance away from us.

"Aye, but it's not what you think." I patted Lorcan's cheek. "We knew each other was out there, but we couldn't get to each other through the locked Veil. Well, I assumed he was dead, but he didn't give up hope."

"Of course not." Lorcan smiled. "Our mate gives us the most hope in our lives."

"I'm sorry I was rude to Pepper to begin with."

Lorcan's smile grew. "I wouldn't expect anything else from you."

Laughing, I hugged him. I loved his sass even though it clashed with mine. That's what family was though, the ones we loved and cherished even when they annoyed us.

We'd fix the spring. I couldn't lose any of them.

# CHAPTER THIRTY-ONE
## AISLINN

FALLON WALKED WITH ME to my bed chambers and collapsed face-first on the bed. Groaning, he rolled over and then crooked his finger at me. I climbed over him, laying my head on his chest, he wrapped his arms around my back and held me close. Every second with him like this was so right and perfect.

Well, almost perfect.

If it wasn't for our life-threatening fears, that was.

"We'll fix it," he said.

"I think so too," I said back, raising my head and meeting his eyes. "Thank you for never giving up on me."

He rubbed my back. "Never. We'll have our eternity. I'm sure of it."

"If anyone deserves forever, it's us." I smiled, then yawned. "Dia, I'm so tired." I lifted the potion in my hand. "Are you willing to drink a witch's potion?"

"I'm willing to do anything for you." He collected the potion bottle from my hand. "One drop?"

I nodded my head. "I can't believe I'm trusting a witch."

"Magic is only bad in the hands of evil."

I cupped his cheek. "My wise mate."

He snorted a laugh. "I wasn't wise letting you go."

"You have me now for however long that is, and that's all that matters."

"I want our forever."

I leaned forward and kissed him. The desperation behind the kiss intensified at the notion of losing him.

"Hey," he whispered, brushing his thumbs over my eyelids capturing the moisture welling there. "I believe in you. In us. We'll have our forever. I promise."

"I want to believe." My bottom lip trembled.

"Then believe."

"So simple?" I raised an eyebrow.

"It is." He placed the potion on the bedside table and slid a hand under my dress, stripped off the holster holding the dagger at my ankle.

My skin prickled with awareness of him. His brief touch set me on fire for more. He placed the holster and dagger on the bedside table too and slid my dress higher. Fingertips skated over my skin leaving a trail of goosebumps in their wake. He stripped the other dagger strapped to my thigh. It clunked as it hit the other dagger on the bedside table. A wicked smirk stretched his lips as he drew my dress higher still over my stomach, fingers brushing so close to where I needed him the most. Arousal spiked between us. He shifted letting me experience his erection against my naked thigh through his pants.

"We're supposed to be sleeping but we need this more," he said as his lips met the shell of my ear and tasted the sensitive skin.

Shivers ran through my body.

"Aye, I'll always need you, my love."

"I love you," he said.

"I love you too."

Then his lips were on mine ravishing my mouth. Our love poured between us, flowing now the words were out there. We loved each other. Trusted each other. I didn't think I had it in me, but Fallon had seen me for who I was and loved me. Lips caressed. Tongues twined, sipping, and tasting, setting our desire to the place I longed to go.

I tugged at his shirt until he shrugged out of it leaving his bare chest flattened against mine over my dress. It wasn't enough contact. I struggled with my dress, but Fallon took over and drew the silky fabric over my head. Then his fingers fell to the ribbon on my braid, and he tugged it free.

"I love your hair too," he said as his fingers untangled the long braid until he'd spread the strands over the pillow in a halo. "So beautiful."

Warmth hit my cheeks without warning. He cupped them with his hands then leaned down and kissed me again. The kiss was sweet compared to the last one, but as I threaded my fingers into his hair, the kiss turned ragged along with our breaths. He reached between us, stroking the aching mounds of my breasts until my nipples were hard with anticipation. His fingers tugged and pinched the hard peaks until a ragged moan left my throat.

"You even sound beautiful."

"Fallon," I sighed his name, part in frustration, part in awe he made me feel so special, so treasured. So loved.

His mouth swooped to my straining nipples and sucked them into the warmth. My back bowed off the bed as a jolt of pleasure shot straight to my core. I rubbed against his straining erection, desperate to have him inside me now and forever. My hands found his pants and tugged at them until he took the hint and tore them off before falling back between my legs, his thick erection rubbing the slickness of my core but not sliding inside.

My fingernails scored his back. His head reared back as his lust-filled gaze stared back at me. He snatched my hands and pinned them to the pillow above my head, then with a swift move I didn't see coming, he thrust inside me.

My power flared in my hands making the room glow a pretty purple hue and making this moment even more magical than it was. He rolled his hips sending the length of his cock deep inside me and hitting nerve endings that were alive with pleasure. Over and over, he pounded into me, each stroke hitting me in the right way to take me closer to orgasm.

Above my head, a soft glow emanated from his palms. His power joined with mine in a way that was so right I wanted to let it free. Let the sensation overwhelm me, but Fallon ground his hips harder, hitting my clit with an accuracy that had me seeing stars in a room that shouldn't have stars.

My breath stuck in my lungs. The beauty on Fallon's face was something to behold, but the beauty of our connection made my heart race inside my chest. Fated mates were special and now I'd found that connection, I wouldn't let it go. I curled my fingers over Fallon's hands and held onto him as the pending orgasm raced to the top of the peak. Everything in the world stopped.

There was only him and me.

Connected in this beautiful moment.

We fell together. Hips grinding as our orgasms exploded in perfect sync. Spasm after spasm of pleasure swallowed my body whole and kept me there in that blissful place. Fallon dropped his lips to mine and held them there for what felt like a very long time. When my breathing returned to normal, and my heart beat at a steady pace, Fallon rolled over taking me with him and urging my head to his chest.

He picked up the potion bottle, uncorked it then held the dropper to my mouth. I opened my mouth accepting the potion and trusting my mate. He lifted the dropper to his mouth and swallowed a drop.

Fallon placed the potion on the side table next to my daggers, and said, "Sweet dreams."

# CHAPTER THIRTY-TWO
# FALLON

As the potion pulled me toward sleep, I ran my fingers through Aislinn's hair. I'd never get enough of her silky strands, but she always had them tied in that tight braid that made me want to tug it free.

I wanted her free and happy.

For the rest of her life, I'd see to it, and I meant what I said, that I believed we'd find a solution to the Fae problems. I believed we'd have forever together.

There was no other option.

My fingers stilled. Sleep swamped me, but instead of falling into a dreamless sleep, Aislinn stood before me gloriously naked.

"So far, I love this dream," I said.

Aislinn laughed. "I believe this is my dream."

I rushed toward her, catching her in my arms and swinging her around, then and only then did I realize I was completely naked too.

"What is this?" she asked.

"I'd say the potion," I said, grinning. "I'll have to thank Pepper when we wake."

Aislinn laughed again. Dia, her laughter was the best thing about her, and she didn't do it enough. I'd make her laugh more in the future.

"Do you think we can sleep like this all the time?" I asked, sweeping kisses over her neck.

"No idea." She giggled as I hit a sensitive spot that made her squirm too.

"I always dreamed of you even when we weren't together, but this is so much better."

She caught my chin with her hand. "You dreamed of me?"

"Always and forever," I said.

I kissed her, pouring the emotions I held deep in my heart into the connection between us in this dream. A dream where we were together.

The only difference was this dream was real.

My mate was here. My mate loved me.

We'd have our always and forever.

## Fated Mates of the Fae Royals

1. Fae's Song

2. Fae's Wolf

3. Fae's Alpha

4. Fae's Heart

5. Fae's Witch

6. Fae's Dream

7. Fae's Fate

8. Fae's Love

# Acknowledgments

First, thank you to my family for putting up with me disappearing into the world of books. To Belinda, thank you for encouraging me to write again after I lost everything in a computer crash. Remember to back up! A lot of work goes into creating a story, and I'm always thankful for the support of my online writing buddies, beta readers, and fellow authors, Immy for always making me smile, Tammy for believing in me from the start, Heather and Cassie for their help, Lana for her invaluable knowledge. The biggest thank you goes to my 'twin' Dannielle, who is the best critique partner, cheerleader, and sounding board ever, and is forever fixing my comma errors, sorry Dannielle I'm afraid you're stuck with them and me. Finally thank you to all you romance readers. You are my tribe.

# ALSO BY

FANTASY AND PARANORMAL ROMANCE
**Summer Court**
Fae's Song
Fae's Wolf
Fae's Alpha
Fae's Heart
Fae's Witch
Fae's Dream
Fae's Fate
Fae's Love

Cᴏɴᴛᴇᴍᴘᴏʀᴀʀʏ Rᴏᴍᴀɴᴄᴇ
**Billionaires' Reluctant Brides**
Their Love Deal
His Pleasure Contract
Love Negotiations
Her Love Submission

**Hollywood Hearts Short Stories**
How The Grinch Lusted After Santa
Lusting After Valentine
The Lustful Leprechaun
The Lust Bunny
Lustman To The Rescue
The Lust Giving

**Hope Bay**
Moving On With Mr. Fix It
Falling For Mr. Faking It

**Anthologies**
Reluctant Bride
Alpha Male

# ABOUT AUTHOR

Helen Walton is a tea drinking, chocoholic, romance writer. Stories are her obsession. She adores creating sensual romances containing a sprinkling of humor and the all-important happy ending. She lives in South Australia with her family, and menagerie of quirky animals where they all take her away from her book world and demand to be fed. Lucky for them, she enjoys cooking but prefers baking.

Sign up for my newsletter for exclusive content.
https://www.helenwaltonauthor.com/newsletter